ANNE PETERS

Twice a RITA finalist
A Golden Heart finalist

"Ms. Peters superbly showcases the
power of love and forgiveness."
—*Romantic Times*

"Excellent romance reading."
—*Rendezvous*

"...a striking intensity to her appealing
characterizations makes this love story something
special."
—*Romantic Times*

"Don't miss this one!"
—*Rendezvous*

"Anne Peters imbues her emotionally intense love
story with a subtle sensuality that discerning
readers will greatly appreciate."
—*Romantic Times*

"A gripping, emotional read..."
—*Rendezvous*

D0958816

Dear Reader,

July brings you the fifth title of Silhouette Romance's VIRGIN BRIDES promotion. This series is devoted to the beautiful metaphor of the traditional white wedding and the fairy-tale magic of innocence awakened to passionate love on the wedding night. In perennial favorite Sandra Steffen's offering, *The Bounty Hunter's Bride,* a rugged loner finds himself propositioned by the innocent beauty who'd nursed him to health in a remote mountain cabin. He resists her precious gift...but winds up her shotgun groom when her father and four brothers discover their hideaway!

Diana Whitney returns to the Romance lineup with *One Man's Promise,* a wonderfully warmhearted story about a struggling FABULOUS FATHER and an adventurous single gal who are brought together by their love for his little girl and a shaggy mutt named Rags. And THE BRUBAKER BRIDES are back! In *Cinderella's Secret Baby,* the third book of Carolyn Zane's charming series, tycoon Mac Brubaker tracks down the poor but proud bride who'd left him the day after their whirlwind wedding, only to discover she's about to give birth to the newest Brubaker heir....

Wanted: A Family Forever is confirmed bachelor Zach Robinson's secret wish in this intensely emotional story by Anne Peters. But will marriage-jaded Monica Griffith and her little girl trust him with their hearts? Linda Varner's twentieth book for Silhouette is book two of THREE WEDDINGS AND A FAMILY. When two go-getters learn they must marry to achieve their dreams, a wedding of convenience results in a *Make-Believe Husband*...and many sleepless nights! Finally, a loyal assistant agrees to be her boss's *Nine-to-Five Bride* in Robin Wells's sparkling new story, but of course this wife wants her new husband to be a *permanent* acquisition!

Enjoy each and every Silhouette Romance!

Regards,

Joan Marlow Golan

Joan Marlow Golan
Senior Editor Silhouette Books

Please address questions and book requests to:
Silhouette Reader Service
U.S.: 3010 Walden Ave., P.O. Box 1325, Buffalo, NY 14269
Canadian: P.O. Box 609, Fort Erie, Ont. L2A 5X3

WANTED:
A FAMILY FOREVER

Anne Peters

Silhouette
ROMANCE™
Published by Silhouette Books
America's Publisher of Contemporary Romance

If you purchased this book without a cover you should be aware
that this book is stolen property. It was reported as "unsold and
destroyed" to the publisher, and neither the author nor the
publisher has received any payment for this "stripped book."

To my agent, Karen Solem, for being so very supportive
and understanding. And to my editor,
Mary-Theresa Hussey, for nudging my sometimes
wayward creativity into marketable channels.
Thank you, ladies. Very much.

 SILHOUETTE BOOKS

ISBN 0-373-19309-2

WANTED: A FAMILY FOREVER

Copyright © 1998 by Anne Hansen

All rights reserved. Except for use in any review, the reproduction
or utilization of this work in whole or in part in any form by any
electronic, mechanical or other means, now known or hereafter
invented, including xerography, photocopying and recording, or in
any information storage or retrieval system, is forbidden without
the written permission of the editorial office, Silhouette Books,
300 East 42nd Street, New York, NY 10017 U.S.A.

All characters in this book have no existence outside the imagination of
the author and have no relation whatsoever to anyone bearing the same
name or names. They are not even distantly inspired by any individual
known or unknown to the author, and all incidents are pure invention.

This edition published by arrangement with Harlequin Books S.A.

® and TM are trademarks of Harlequin Books S.A., used under license.
Trademarks indicated with ® are registered in the United States Patent
and Trademark Office, the Canadian Trade Marks Office and in other
countries.

Printed in U.S.A.

Books by Anne Peters

Silhouette Romance

Through Thick and Thin #739
Next Stop: Marriage #803
And Daddy Makes Three #821
Storky Jones Is Back in Town #850
Nobody's Perfect #875
The Real Malloy #899
The Pursuit of Happiness #927
Accidental Dad #946
His Only Deception #995
McCullough's Bride #1031
*Green Card Wife #1104
*Stand-in Husband #1110
*Along Comes Baby #1116
My Baby, Your Son #1222
Love, Marriage and Family 101 #1254
Wanted: A Family Forever #1309

Silhouette Desire

Like Wildfire #497

*First Comes Marriage

ANNE PETERS

Anne Peters shares her Pacific Northwest home with her husband, Manfred, and a lovable rottweiler named Gisela who takes Anne for walks three times a day. Writing, reading, family, friends and the sound of the ocean—this, to Anne, is happiness.

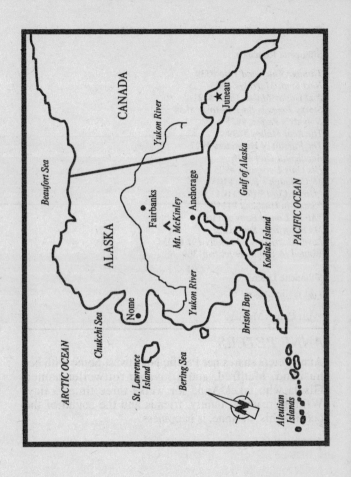

Chapter One

The North Star Hotel Welcomes Brides For Alaska.

Hurrying past the reader board toward the hotel, Monica Griffith glanced at the glittering message with an inward groan. She asked herself, not for the first time, how something that had once seemed like such a fun idea could have become such a burden.

The answer, of course, was that during the year and some months since its inception, her world had spun off its axis and been dangerously out of kilter ever since. The happily-ever-afters of strangers had, as a consequence, become a matter of disinterest to her. Something much more vital demanded all of her energies now. Her own safety and that of her child. Nicole.

Both for the present as well as the future, the well-being of that one little girl had to take priority over everything else.

She wouldn't be at this function at all, would already be well on her way to Kodiak if she hadn't felt obligated to honor at least this one small part of her commitment to a woman who had been nothing but understanding. A woman who had no knowledge of Monica's travails, but who had asked no questions.

Skirting a puddle, Monica sighed. She liked and respected Rebecca Sanders and wanted to confide in her. But it was too risky. Just being here tonight was dangerous enough, especially with Nicky as sick as she was.

Zach Robinson exited the North Star Hotel with every intention of making a getaway while he still could. He did not desire a bride and had been a fool to let his sister coerce him into coming to this shindig in the first place. One glance into the ballroom, where clumps of women of all shapes and sizes hovered on the opposite side from clumps of equally ill-at-ease men, and where Becky had thankfully not yet been in evidence, had been enough to make him turn on his heel and run the other way.

Outside, he winced at the message on the oversize reader board—Brides For Alaska. What a concept! He noted that the leggy blonde rushing toward him seemed to feel the same.

"Hoaky, isn't it?" he remarked with a nod toward the sign as they came abreast of each other. He didn't usually talk to strange young women in parking lots; the words just sort of popped out of their own volition. He expected a responding nod, perhaps even a smile of agreement. But what he got was silence and a startled almost wary glance as the woman swished past him with coattails flying. She disappeared inside the hotel with a forceful spin of the revolving door.

Zach stared after her, brows raised. He hadn't meant to give offense but it certainly seemed to have been taken. He wondered if she might be one of the so-called brides and, understandably, from his point of view, feeling self-conscious about it.

He sighed. His reluctance to make like a desperate bachelor for the sake of family peace hadn't lessened, but it occurred to him that if even just a few of the women at his sister's function were as good-looking as the one he'd just encountered, maybe the evening wouldn't be a total loss, after all.

Squaring his shoulders, Zach caught the door that had whizzed by twice from the force of the lady's entry and followed her back inside.

It was warm in the lobby after the brisk August night outside where rain, the chilly, autumny kind, was definitely in the air. Summers tended to be short in Anchorage, Alaska.

Glancing around the elegantly furnished reception area of the grand old hotel, the legendary Iditerod Lounge drew Zach's eyes. He fleetingly reflected that in another lifetime he would have ducked in there for a shot or two or three of liquid fortitude before making an appearance at this Brides thing he dreaded.

But these days that was no longer an option. And he couldn't, in all honesty, even lament that anymore. He supposed that meant he'd finally grown up. Too bad he'd had to grow *old* before achieving that....

The reception, he reminded himself, and removed his light raincoat. Wondering where he could check it, he spotted the woman from the parking lot at the lobby's far end, near the open doors to the ballroom. She, too, was shedding her coat, but talking into one of the pay phones there at the same time. Zach figured she must have made a beeline for the thing immediately upon entering.

To lodge a complaint about being ''accosted'' by him in the parking lot? Zach inwardly grimaced, thinking surely not, though anything was possible in these days of political correctness paranoia. Certainly the glance she now tossed him before presenting him with her profile was anything but cordial.

He probably should be looking for the cloakroom instead of watching her, but something about her arrested him. Clearly, she was troubled. Her features, in profile, were delicately carved, but marred by her downcast expression. He could have sworn that her hand shook as she dragged a shimmering fall of sun-streaked hair off her face after carelessly dropping her coat onto a nearby chair. Her head was bent, her eyes on the carpet.

She wasn't young, Zach decided, though certainly too young for him. Early to mid-thirties, he'd hazard, which would make her a dozen years or more his junior. The majority of the women he'd glimpsed in the ballroom seemed to be, age-wise, similarly in that bracket. He ought to put his coat back on and leave.

But he didn't. He stood where he was and let his gaze slide downward, taking in the woman's shape and apparel. Black dress. Simple, but stylish. Party-time stylish. Which had to mean she was one of the quote-unquote brides. She was also, he admitted, decidedly one of the "lookers" Becky had bragged about in her arm-twisting phone call. Her clingy little dress lovingly draped the kind of figure any healthy male would look at twice.

Knowing himself to be in the best of health in spite of his forty-six years and graying temples, Zach didn't hesitate to appreciatively look his fill. He decided that if he were younger and less emotionally crippled, she would definitely have the stuff to spark a deeper interest. As it was, however, his interest in her was strictly short-term and superficial.

It was based on the fact that her expression and demeanor as she talked on the phone seemed to indicate she was no happier to be here than he was. Which led him to speculate if maybe she'd been manipulated into attending this affair, too. And if so, that maybe she'd appreciate being "rescued" by someone like him, someone who had no ulterior motive except to make the best of a bad situation for a few hours.

They could make an appearance inside the ballroom together, just long enough for Rebecca to see them and be appeased, and then they could split. In separate directions, of course.

It seemed like the perfect plan.

She was being watched.

Trying to concentrate on what her mother was saying, Monica could practically *feel* somebody's eyes drilling into her. Instantly wary, she glanced toward the middle of the lobby and felt the blood drain from her face when she saw it was the man who'd made that mocking comment about the reader board message outside the hotel. Dear God. Could Richard have hired somebody to...

Stop it, Monica told herself firmly. It was too soon. And anyway, Richard had no knowledge of her mother's new last name and whereabouts, and he'd never shown enough interest in her business affairs to know about this Alaska Brides thing.

Besides, she was still alive enough as a woman to recognize that the man's protracted regard, while unnerving in its unwavering intensity, was appreciative rather than threatening.

Still, she averted her eyes in pointed dismissal, turning her back as she asked, "Are you sure, Mom, that her temp is down?"

She strained to listen to her mother's reply over the cacophony of sound emitting from the ballroom where the cocktail reception was in full swing. Once again she fervently wished she didn't have to be here tonight.

Because Nicole had the flu. A minor thing for other five-year-olds, perhaps, but for someone like Nicole just one more thing to cope with on top of everything that had gone before. From the pre- and post-divorce battles between Richard and herself to the drama and trauma of the past several weeks, it had just been one relentless succession of nightmares for her little girl.

Today's flight from Seattle to Anchorage had further terrified the child, and their temporary home at the modest motel down the street from the Arctic Circle was just one more unfamiliar room to adjust to. This in spite of the fact that her Gramma Carla, whom she had come to love and, more importantly, trust, was there with her.

Not that she cried, or even complained. If only she would.

"Ninety-nine point five is still up, Mom," Monica exhorted fretfully. "Did you get her to swallow the aspirins? Well, try the liquid, then. All right. Give her a kiss and tell her I'll be home as soon as I can."

Her parting, "'Bye" hardly more than a shivery sigh, Monica hung up the phone. With her back to the lobby and her mind on her child, she took a few bracing breaths to compose herself.

You can do this, she told herself, and started when a masculine voice from behind her said, "Excuse me."

She jerked around. Stiffened. *That man again.*

She hadn't noticed him coming closer; they were only a couple of feet apart. She frowned up at him. He was very tall. And his face, at this close distance, bore a remarkable resemblance to Walter Matthau's as he'd looked some twenty years ago.

The smile he offered was charming. And disconcertingly disarming.

Monica steeled herself against it. She didn't want to like this man. Didn't want to like any man, anywhere. Ever again.

"Yes?" she asked coolly. Only the thought that he could, just possibly, be one of Rebecca Sanders's clients was stopping her from simply walking away. "Can I help you?"

"I certainly hope so." His voice was a pleasantly resonant baritone that somehow managed to sound authoritative and persuasive at the same time. "You see, I need a companion."

"Oh." Good thing she hadn't been rude. "Then you *are* one of the bachelors?"

"Why?" he asked. His eyes, their color the palest blue she had ever seen, twinkled with humor and his deepening smile made the myriad creases in his tanned and decidedly lived-in face settle into even deeper grooves. "Is that a requirement?"

"It is if you want my assistance."

"I see." Zach's interest in the woman deepened. He wondered why she made such a point of being bristly. After all, wasn't the purpose of this shindig to make a connection? "Perhaps I'm going about this the wrong way," he said apologetically. "My name is Robinson. Zach Robinson." He offered his hand.

Monica pretended not to notice. She indicated the ballroom. "The reception is in there, Mr. Robinson. And so are any number of potential companions."

Zach smiled, thinking, *She's got you there, pal.* But he hadn't gotten to where he was in life by being easily discouraged, and something about her very reticence made him want to persevere.

"Call me Zach," he said. "And to tell you the truth, I was hoping that you—"

"Zacharius!"

Becky. Damn her lousy timing....

Swallowing a sigh, and murmuring, "Excuse me," to Monica, Zach turned to watch his sister bounce toward him. As compact and tiny as he was rangy and tall, Rebecca's inexhaustible enthusiasm preceded her like a tangible force.

"You came," she exclaimed with a brief one-armed squeeze around his middle. The top of her head barely reached his shoulder. "I just knew you wouldn't let me down."

She beamed at Monica. "And you. Thanks a million."

"You're welcome," Monica said.

But Becky's attention had already reverted to Zach. "What're you still doing out here? The party's in there."

"So I've been told." Zach exchanged a glance with

Monica before smiling down at his sister. Though he should still be angry with her for blackmailing him into this thing, and though he wished she hadn't discovered his presence for another couple of minutes at least, he loved her too dearly to hold a grudge. Becky was and always had been his best friend, his champion, his rock. He owed her a lot.

He dropped a kiss on the top of her salt-'n'-peppery hair. "I was mingling."

"Mingling?" Rebecca rolled her eyes at Monica, who shrugged, happy to have the man off her hands without really caring who or what.

"Talking to Monica out here in the lobby is not *mingling*," Rebecca said firmly. "Now come on. I need you inside. Both of you."

"Just let me take my coat to the cloakroom," Monica said.

"Me, too," Zach said quickly, and tried to disengage himself from Becky.

She wouldn't have it. "Monica will take it," she said, taking the coat off Zach's arm and thrusting it at Monica. "You don't mind, do you, dear?" She winked. "I don't trust this guy out of my sight."

Once again Monica's eyes met Zach's. Their hunted expression was really quite comical. "I'll bring you the claim check," she said.

"Thank you, but—" *I'd just as soon take care of this myself,* Zach was going to say.

But Becky was already hauling him toward the ballroom with surprising strength for one so small.

Zach stifled an oath and sent a chagrined and apologetic glance back to Monica. Her smile of amusement caught him unawares. She was lovely when she smiled. And that loveliness made his breath catch and his steps falter.

Becky stopped, too. Just long enough to call, "Hurry, Monica dear. I really need you to help keep things moving."

Monica, her smile fading, raised a hand in acknowledgment and briskly strode toward the coat check. Zach, reluctantly trailing his sister but still casting back glances, couldn't help but admire the sway of her hips.

"Nice young woman," he remarked. "Monica, her name is?"

"Hmm."

"She work for you?"

"Nuh-uh." Becky had stopped moving and was scanning the dimly lit ballroom.

Following suit, Zach's overall impression was of a blur of faceless men and women whose undulating drone of voices was punctuated by an occasional giggle and backed up by a piped-in Muzac system.

"Are we looking for anyone in particular?" he asked, wondering just how quickly he could get back to Monica. "Because if not—"

"There she is!" Becky dragged him toward the left side of the room.

"Who?"

"The woman I want you to meet." She sliced him meaningful look. "I think you'll agree that she's exactly what you're looking for."

Looking for? Zach planted his feet. He glared down at his sister. "Rebecca, so help me—"

"Hush." Rebecca glanced around, keeping a bright, professional smile on her lips as she chided, "You agreed to be nice."

"I agreed to show up," Zach corrected before recalling that he hadn't even done that. She'd coerced him by threatening to never speak to him again and then slamming down the phone. The trick had worked because she and her husband and kids were all the family he had, and because he alone knew how much hell she had gone through to look out for him, growing up. And since.

Well, he was here, but he'd be damned if he'd let her

dictate with whom he'd spend his time. "I've already picked out the companion I want."

"Who? Monica?" his sister had the nerve to laughingly inquire. "If she was the companion you had in mind, darling, you can just think again."

"Why? Because you've already got someone else picked out for her, too? I thought people are supposed to find *each other* at this affair. And that you run a computer *dating* business, not a matchmaking institute."

"Are you through?" Rebecca sweetly asked in a tone of great patience. A clear sign that her temper was gathering steam.

Given their surroundings, Zach thought it best to ease off. "I await your rebuttal," he said with a slightly pained grin.

Which his sister returned, saying, "Spoken like a lawyer."

"Purely unintentional, I assure you."

"More's the pity." She caught his eye and waved the comment away. "Sorry. We were talking about Monica Griffith who, as I started to explain, is not for you. Not only because she is definitely *out of* the marriage market, but also because she just happens to be my partner in this affair. Monica is—*was*—the liaison, as it were, between our worthy bachelors up here and the lovely ladies of the lower forty-eight. *Comprende?*"

She was dragging him along by the arm again without waiting for a reply. Zach figured that his dour expression had probably been answer enough.

He also wondered, while letting Rebecca herd him toward a colorful cluster of women, why it should bother him that this Monica was, so to speak, off the market.

He looked around for her, only to have Becky give his arm a sharp tug. "Zach, dear, say hello to Heather Monroe."

"Hello." Zach obediently greeted the rather outdoorsy-looking blonde who was gazing up at him with a discomfiting mixture of lust and awe.

"Heather's an environmental activist," Rebecca attested, while Zach wondered just how quickly he could make good an escape. "She's from Olympia, Washington. Now, isn't that a coincidence?"

Zach squirmed as two sets of eyes—one belonging to his sister—adoringly gazed up at him. "Before retiring to Alaska," Rebecca further annoyed him by saying, "Zach used to argue environmental issues in front of the legislature there in Washington State."

Another sharp tug on the arm. "Didn't you, Zach?"

"Er, yes." Zach managed to free his abused limb from his sister's clutch while shooting her a quelling glare. What was she playing at, dragging his past life into this introduction?

"It's been years, though," he said grimly. "And to tell you the truth—"

"Oh, this is *such* a pleasure," the woman called Heather interrupted ecstatically. She grabbed his right hand in both of hers and pumped it up and down. "I can't say that I recall your environmental activities, but I used to be *such* a fan of yours, in your basketball playing days. I was a freshman in college when you were the Sonics's star forward...."

Dear God. Shutting out the woman's delighted babble, Zach met his sister's now remorseful gaze with an expression that clearly said, *Get me out of this. Now.*

Becky redeemed herself somewhat in his eyes by instantly latching on to the sleeve of the first man passing by and dragging him into their circle.

"Leonard," she said brightly. "Leonard Jenkins, have you met Heather Monroe? Lenny's in logging—he's *vastly* wealthy," she added for Heather's ears only in a whispered aside. Then louder again, "I think you two'll find a lot to talk about.

"Yoo-hoo, Anna," she trilled, wiggling her fingers as

she urged Zach toward another group that, he was relieved to note, already included several men. "Sorry, Zach," she said under her breath. "I didn't think."

"S'okay." He returned the squeeze of her fingers. "Just please keep in mind that I'm here only as a favor to you. I'm not a candidate."

"More's the pity," Becky murmured once again, but this time Zach pretended not to hear.

Watching events from the other side of the room, Monica could almost feel sorry for the man. He was clearly not here of his own volition; but then Rebecca Sanders, for all she was barely five feet tall, could be a formidable force. No doubt she had called in a few favors when, at the last minute, the bachelor list had come up short.

Wondering in spite of herself if he was a relative of Becky's or a friend, Monica saw him glance around searchingly as he was towed along from group to group like a dancing bear on a leash. As his rumpled face creased still more deeply into an expression of grim resignation, she felt a definite tug of sympathy.

And when his eyes chanced to encounter hers and took on an expression of almost desperate entreaty, Monica was hard put not to respond to it by coming to his rescue. Which was as annoying a notion as it was ridiculous. The man was more than capable of looking out for himself, while she had enough troubles on her plate already without adding any more.

She stopped a passing waiter and handed him the claim check. After pointing Zach out to him, she thought, There. Now that's that.

That was not quite that, as it turned out, because they came face-to-face again a couple of hours later. To Zach it had seemed an eternity before he'd finally managed to extricate himself from the clutch of females that was by

that time surrounding him. Several of the older bachelor-
ettes had recognized him as the bad boy of basketball he'd
been two decades ago. He couldn't wait to get out of that
ballroom and, apparently realizing he'd do or say something regrettable if she didn't let him leave, Becky had not
said a word when he'd curtly announced, "It's been a
pleasure, ladies, but duty calls."

He hadn't explained what *duty*. There wasn't any; he'd
simply had enough. He strode out into the lobby to find
Monica just hanging up the phone.

"Another call?" he queried sourly while blotting his
brow with his handkerchief. He stuffed it into his pocket
and scowled at her. He'd been disappointed when a waiter
instead of her had brought him the claim ticket. "Checking
in with hubby?"

"Making good your escape?" Monica countered, and
looked at him askance as he simply fell into step beside
her.

"Would it matter if I did?"

"Not to me." Monica was leaving. Nicole was feeling
worse and wouldn't settle, her mother had told her over
the phone. Rebecca had assured her, albeit not too happily,
that she could manage the rest of the evening on her own.
"I'm going home."

"Ah." Zach glanced down at her and their eyes met
once again. Though Monica was sure hers hadn't asked
the question, he nevertheless elaborated, "Rebecca is my
sister."

"I see."

"She made me come," Zach said. They were at the coat
check and had surrendered their tickets. Waiting, their
glances chanced to once more connect.

"I'm kind of glad now I did," Zach said. Almost ab-
sently, because he'd been struck, suddenly, by the sadness
that lurked in Monica's eyes as well as by the way their
hazel color seemed to change in tandem with her facial

expressions. He almost remarked on it, then decided that would be overreaching himself.

Especially since she hadn't said one way or the other if her phone calls had been to a husband. Not that it was really his business, or even relevant. In a few more minutes they'd be going their separate ways and that would be that.

"Quite a party," he said, ingrained good manners making him reach for her coat, which she relinquished after a short tug-of-war. "And a darned good idea, really. My earlier gibe at the reader board notwithstanding," he added with a grin.

To which she didn't respond.

He helped her into the coat. Though he had no business doing so, his eyes admired the heavy swath of silky hair she tugged free of the garment as it settled on her shoulders. A subtle whiff of some flowery scent accompanied the gesture.

Because it made him want to close his eyes and bury his face in it, he took a step back.

When she faced him, fastening buttons, he asked, just to say something, "You weren't having a good time?"

"No, I wasn't," she said. "Not that that's relevant, since I was here to work."

"Right. You're Becky's partner." He accepted his own coat from the attendant and tossed some bills on the counter after putting it on. "So what're you doing in the dating business?"

"At this point in time? Getting out of it. For good." Coat buttoned, Monica picked up her handbag and took out her wallet.

"Please—" Zach forestalled her opening it "—I got it."

"Thanks, but no thanks," Monica said firmly. She gave the woman a dollar bill. "Good night, Mr. Robinson."

"Zach," he corrected her again. He walked with her to the revolving door, casting a glance through the floor-to-ceiling windows on either side. "It's pouring rain out there."

"So I see."

"Your car—"

"I'm on foot."

"You *walked?*"

"Yes." She turned up the collar of her light coat. "It's not far."

"Anywhere's too far in this soaker." Zach resolutely squeezed into the revolving triangle with her. Their shoulders and hips bumped as they pushed their way outside. "I'll drive you."

She glared up at him. "No, you won't."

It was raining so hard, she had to raise her voice above the sound of it.

He just glanced at her speakingly and, gripping her elbow, gave her no choice but to keep up or be dragged as, head lowered against the driving rain, he trotted to his car. It was parked nearby, a roomy Suburban, as apparently well-used and unpretentious as this nevertheless irritatingly high-handed man who was shoving her into the passenger seat with all the finesse of a teamster tossing a crate of cargo.

And who shook himself like a wet dog after collapsing into the driver's seat. "You were planning to walk in *this?*"

Blotting at her face with a tissue, Monica sliced him a glare through soggy lashes. "I would hardly have gotten much wetter than I am now."

"Wanna bet?" With a sound of impatience, Zach started the car and backed out of the slot. "Where to?"

"The Greenbriar. Turn right at the street, then—"

"I know where it is." He scowled at her. "It's a fleabag."

"Hardly that."

"It's second rate." He pulled into traffic. There wasn't much of it. "Who recommended it?"

"Your sister."

"Oh." Their gazes collided. Monica's resentful; Zach's chagrined.

Monica jerked her eyes away and stared straight ahead as humiliation and affront made her do a slow burn.

"Look, I'm sorry," Zach said. He knew himself to be many things, but an insensitive jackass he wasn't. At least, not usually. As to his sister, she would never have recommended the place if a better, pricier hotel had been an option. Money was obviously tight. "Your husband out of work?"

She didn't want to answer him. He could tell by the way her nostrils flared and her hands closed into fists on her lap.

"My *husband*," she finally said in a voice rough with strain and emotion, "is out, period."

"I see." Damn, they were there already. Grimly, Zach pulled into the yard, past the Greenbriar sign with a third of its letters burned out. Grinding his back teeth in frustration because suddenly there seemed a hundred things he wanted to ask that he knew she wouldn't want to answer, he eased the Suburban through the narrow strip of asphalt fronting a row of one-storied dreariness.

"Which unit?"

"Twelve." Monica sat tall and regal as a queen when he pulled into the space in front of her door. Dignity. She clung to it like a drowning person to a life preserver, knowing it was all she had in front of this man. This stranger who, for all he was irksome and overbearing, had about him an air of kindness and steadfastness that made her long to curl up in his arms because she intuitively knew she'd be safe there.

Which was precisely why, when he killed the engine and turned toward her, she couldn't get out of the car and away from him fast enough. "Thanks for the ride."

"Forget it."

She fumbled with the door handle, couldn't make it

work. She gasped, shrinking into herself for an instant of mindless panic when he leaned toward her. She felt his breath on her face and held her own as their shoulders touched and his hand reached out.

Reached out and past her to open the door. He pushed it wide and sat back.

"Good night, Ms. Griffith," he said, his tone clipped now, and his expression hard. Clearly he had noted, and felt insulted by, her reaction to his proximity.

She stood in the rain and their eyes still clung. Feeling foolish about her behavior, Monica would have liked to explain about the precarious state of her emotions.

But in the end all she said was, "Goodbye, Mr. Robinson."

Chapter Two

"Here, let me carry that," Zach said gruffly, and took the bulging duffel bag out of his querulous old housekeeper's calloused hand. He grunted. "What you got in there anyway? Gold bullion?"

"Don't I wish." Ada Gordon smacked her toothless gums—she only wore her dentures at mealtimes—before exposing them, pink and gleaming as a baby's, in a smile that was mean more than humorous, but one hundred percent Ada. "Since I wouldn't need to be puttin' up with the likes o' you then."

"Likes o' me, is it?" Zach cocked an eye toward the rain-lashed terminal windows of Homer Airport. Ada's daughter-in-law had dropped her off there to rendezvous with him for the flight home to Kodiak. "Nice day out there for a boat ride," he teased, deadpan. "Plenty of time for you to get over to the ferry terminal if you're so anxious to be away from the *likes o' me*."

Ada's only reply was a snort and a sniff.

"Hear the Dramamine Run'll depart in about an hour." Zach continued to bait her.

As expected, she didn't bite. "Ridin' that *Tustamena* couldn't be no worse'n flying with you in that crate you call an airplane," she told him with another snort.

It was Sunday. After spending a miserable Saturday dodging his sister's phone calls by hanging out at Northern Air, the Anchorage F.B.O. where he always tied down his plane, he had been more than glad to leave the city behind. He'd flown the short hop to Homer this morning and was even glad now to have Ada back to spar with.

Standing next to him by the window, she gestured to an approaching Alaska Airlines flight. "Why, lookit the way that there big bird's coming down. Ooh-ee."

"Must be a new pilot." Though he spoke dismissively, still bantering, Zach carefully watched the 737's wobbly approach. The wind seemed definitely to have picked up since he'd put down forty minutes ago.

"Meaning you can do better," Ada said dryly.

"You know I can."

"Yeah." Ada straightened her kerchief, serious now. "Wouldn't get me up there with you otherwise. Here, hold this…" She handed him her remaining, smaller bag. "I've gotta go freshen up."

"Right." Zach set down both of her bags and, after watching her waddle to the ladies' rest room, checked his watch. Eleven-thirty. He hoped Ada wouldn't be too long "freshening." He went to the phone a few feet away and checked on weather conditions one more time. As he'd suspected, there was a front coming in. But he was told that he should be well ahead of the system and should have no problems flying his one-eighty-two home to Kodiak.

He'd sure's heck hate to be on that ferryboat, though, Zach reflected. The Gulf could be wicked in a storm.

His call complete, he idly watched the few deplaning passengers from Anchorage file into the terminal. An elderly woman emerged. She looked familiar.

"Hey, ain't that Mrs. Romanov?" Ada queried at his elbow.

Zach hadn't noticed Ada's return and didn't acknowledge her now. His attention had been snagged by another woman, a blonde one with legs that seemed to go on forever. And who just happened to be the same young woman who was squarely to blame for his brooding restlessness of the past thirty-odd hours. Bundled up in her arms was a little girl who looked anything but happy.

"Monica?" It wasn't until, startled, Monica swung fearful eyes toward him that Zach realized he had called her name out loud. As she stopped to stare at him, shocked and with dawning recognition, and as warning bells clanged in his head, he strode toward her.

Even pale and distraught, she was, to him, a singularly attractive woman. And whatever it was that had made him so stubbornly latch on to her Friday night, was now prompting him to ask, "What are *you* doing here in Homer?"

It wasn't a very bright question, and the way Monica was looking at him—sort of like she was seeing an unsavory ghost—he was surprised that she even answered. "We're connecting here with the ferry to Kodiak."

"You're kidding! In this weather?"

Her expression grew chill. "When we booked passage, the weather was just fine."

She shifted the child, who had taken one look at Zach and promptly hidden her face in Monica's neck, to her other hip.

"Yours?" he asked.

"Yes." She visibly tightened her arms around the child as though to protect her and he wondered why he didn't do what she obviously wanted him to, namely buzz off and leave her alone. Especially when she said, "I'm afraid you're frightening her."

"I'm sorry," he said stiffly, and did turn away. He was thinking, To hell with her. His face might not be much, but it had never frightened anyone's kids before. But right behind him stood the wife of Pete Romanov, a well-established Kodiak fisherman.

"Carla," he greeted her, good manners making it necessary to mask his pique with civility.

"Zach," she replied with equal formality, darting worried glances toward Monica and the child. "I didn't know you were acquainted with my daughter."

Ah, so *that's* who she is. "I'm not," he said. "At least not very well. She tells me you're headed for the ferry."

"That's right. I'm afraid my granddaughter is real sick and—"

"Mom," Monica interrupted her mother in an urgent tone. "We've got to get going."

"Wait." Zach caught hold of her arm to keep her from walking away, but addressed Carla Romanov. "You can't mean to go through with this. Not in this weather."

Before Monica could speak or stop him, he had gently turned Nicole's head and laid his palm against her forehead. He noted, but didn't remark on, the way the little girl shrank away from his touch. "This child is burning up," he said, glaring first at Monica and then at her mother. "And she ought to be in bed, not on some lumbering ferry for ten stormy hours on the North Pacific."

"It's not your business, Mr. Robinson," Monica said, her expression cool in spite of the wobble in her voice.

Of all the stiff-necked— "Lady, this isn't a walk in the rain here we're arguing about. This child's welfare—"

"Nicole is terrified of flying, Zach," Carla Romanov interrupted in a conciliatory tone.

Zach studied the child who now listlessly stared back at him with unblinking eyes. And he noticed that they were bright with fever. Still... "She looks quiet enough."

"Yes, but that's because she's—" Carla bit her lip and glanced questioningly at her daughter.

Zach saw Monica respond with a quick shake of her head. Her eyes were dark with the kind of pain it would have been impossible for anyone to ignore.

Zach didn't even try. He had endured enough pain of his own to ever knowingly want to inflict any on other people. But he'd once been the parent of a feverish little girl, too. And though it wasn't something he normally talked about, he knew only too well how quickly a young life could be snuffed out when you weren't vigilant.

"Look," he told Monica quietly, reluctantly. "I have no personal stake in this except that once, long ago, I...I *knew* a little girl who... Well, who didn't make it because...well, because she didn't get the care she needed.

"So trust me," he said. "My plane is right outside and ready to go. Let me fly you and your child to Kodiak."

He felt Ada's gnarled hand on his arm. When he glanced at her, she nodded her head approvingly. "Do it," she advised Monica. "I don't mind the ferry ride. Honest. It'll give Mrs. Romanov'n me time to catch up on some gossip."

Her black almond eyes somber and shrewd, she glanced at Carla. "Won't it, dear?"

Carla only nodded, silently entreating her daughter.

"I'm a pretty good pilot," Zach said.

"The best," Ada said firmly.

"My Cessna's a four-seater," Zach said. "You can bed your daughter down on the rear seat, all bundled up. I'll have you in Kodiak in less than an hour."

"Do it," Ada urged again.

"Please, dear," Carla whispered when Monica, still waffling, hugged her child and shook her head in helpless indecision. "He's a good man."

A good man. Monica looked at Zach. Her mother was acquainted with him. And she did want to trust him. But she didn't quite dare. So much was at stake, her entire future. Hers and Nicole's. Just one little error in judgment could jeopardize everything.

But Nicky was sick. Perhaps dangerously so. "She's afraid of airplanes," she said to her mother, to Zach.

She knew it was only one last feeble attempt to avoid

doing what she had vowed never again to do—turn over control of her life, for however short a period of time, to a man.

"All right," she finally capitulated, after weighing the temporary loss of her autonomy against the risk of worsening her child's already alarmingly serious case of the flu. "Looks like I'll have to accept your offer of a ride once again."

"I can't believe she's actually gone to sleep." Monica turned frontward again, whispering into the headset she wore, same as Zach. She voiced what worried her most. "She's awfully hot, though."

"Almost there." Zach switched frequencies and announced his call letters and position, adding, "Get Doc Koontz over to Windemeer. Over."

He dug in his breast pocket and pulled out a stick of gum. "You might want to wake her and give her this to chew while I put this crate down.

"Ears," he elaborated in response to Monica's questioning glance. "Any congestion will make them plug up worse than normal. It hurts."

"Yes, of course. Thank you." Monica peeled off the wrapper, releasing the bracing scent of spearmint into the small space between them. The Cessna's cockpit was cramped. Zach Robinson was big. Not only exceedingly tall, but broad of shoulder and chest. Every movement she or Zach made brought their arms and shoulders into contact. After nearly an hour you'd think she'd have gotten used to it. She hadn't. But she had managed not to visibly shrink away and thus insult him again.

They hadn't said much to each other in the course of the flight. The headsets were constraining, but even more so was Nicole's silent presence in the back seat. Monica wondered what Zach Robinson might be thinking about her and Nicole. He was much too polite to ask, but there had certainly been questions in his eyes at the airport, and since.

Well, let him wonder, Monica thought, awkwardly twisting in her narrow seat to wake her child and give her the gum. I can't afford to confide in anyone, no matter how steady and trustworthy they seem.

Zach's arm grazed her breast as she turned in the seat. This time she did flinch, drawing his gaze. It locked with hers for only a split second and seemed to cause some kind of electricity to arc between them. The sensation was extremely unsettling to Monica, and didn't seem to please Zach a whole lot, either, if his sudden scowl and quickly averted face was anything to go by.

"Nicole, honey," Monica said, trying hard to pretend she'd been oblivious to that flash of tension between Zach and herself. "Wake up, sweetheart. Here's some gum for you..."

She gently shook the unresponsive child, then jerked around in alarm. "She won't wake up." Frantic, she grabbed Zach's arm. "Oh, please, she won't wake up!"

For an instant, panic slammed into Zach, as well. The waking nightmares from long ago came rushing back. Maddy, his sweet little Maddy, limp and unresponsive. And cold, so cold...

But this child isn't cold!

"Monica." Busy with the controls, with lining up for landing, Zach nevertheless spared a moment to cover Monica's icy hand and drill his eyes into hers. "Listen to me. She's feverish. She's deeply asleep, maybe even unconscious. But she's alive. And I'm not, you hear me, *not* gonna let her die."

One more hard look into Monica's eyes and then he had to get back to business or risk all of their welfare. "Hang on now, okay? We're on final approach and I'm going to slide us down smooth as silk and the doctor'll be waiting for us when we get there. I promise."

Numbly, Monica nodded while her hand stole back to

grab hold of her little girl's limp fingers. They were warm, hot. Reassuringly hot. Frighteningly hot. But Zach had promised he wouldn't let Nicole die.

Funny, Monica thought, bracing herself as the Cessna's wheels touched the runway with just the barest bit of a bounce. *But I believe him.*

Zach was cool and in control as they taxied toward the hangar where he could see Deke McBride hustling the tie-downs into place while Mitch Gordon, Ada's youngest, importantly guided the Cessna into her berth with his recently acquired, F.A.A. approved hand signals.

Zach felt even better when he spotted Doc Koontz standing in readiness next to his vintage Mercedes.

He climbed out of the cockpit and briskly rounded the Cessna's nose to help Monica alight on the passenger side. He beckoned to the doctor. "Over here, Doc. Give me a hand.

"She's not responding to stimuli," he whispered to the doctor as they both reached to gently lift the little girl out.

"Let's get her into my car and into the house," was all the doctor said.

The back seat of the grand old Mercedes sedan offered ample comfort to the little figure swathed in blankets.

"I'm coming with you. Wait." Monica, only just realizing that the doctor was about to speed away without her, jumped into the passenger seat and slammed the door.

"Will she be all right?"

"We'll know soon enough, but I'm sure she'll be fine." The doctor, white-haired and bearded just like Saint Nick, reassuringly patted Monica's hand. "Children easily get high fevers. The trick is to get them back down before brain damage occurs."

"I see," Monica said weakly, far from reassured. The workings of Nicole's brain were already such a bewildering mystery to her, the last thing she needed was to have further mayhem done there. "She has the flu."

The doctor gave her a fatherly smile. "Try not to worry so much, my dear."

Easy for you to say. Monica glanced out the window. It struck her then that the place was awfully deserted-looking even for a backwater airport in Alaska.

"Surely this isn't Kodiak airport," she said, unable to keep a note of alarm from creeping into her voice.

"Heavens, no." The doctor laughed. "This is Zach's place. Windemeer."

"So now what's worrying you?" Zach leaned back against the door he'd just closed behind the departing doctor and faced Monica who was fretfully pacing. It was obvious to him that she was exhausted and on the verge of hysteria. And because he suddenly felt an overwhelming desire to enfold her in his arms and soothe her hurts and anxieties away, he kept his tone brisk. "Didn't you hear Doc Koontz say the worst is over? That she's sleeping normally and—"

"That she shouldn't be moved again until she is better!" Monica interrupted, tossing up her hands. "Don't you see how impossible this is?"

"I'm afraid I don't. There's plenty of room and Ada'll be here in just a few more hours." Zach pushed away from the door and headed for the kitchen. "I'm starving. How about you?"

"Starving? Plenty of room?" Monica hurried after him. "What's that got to do with what I'm talking about? We can't just *stay* here until she's better!"

"Why not?" Zach peered into the fridge. He figured the best thing for him to do to diffuse her agitation, as well as keep himself from overreacting to it, was to play it cool. Way cool. "There's ham, cheese, liverwurst…"

"*Liver*wurst?" Monica allowed herself to be side-tracked long enough to shudder.

Zach cocked a brow. He shrugged, saying, "My mother was German," as though that explained it. He dumped it all on the counter, adding tomatoes, pickles and mustard. "Wheat bread or rye?"

When Monica just stared and waved her hands in an agitated fashion, he put down the knife he'd just pulled from the block and said, "Look. Your daughter is sick. And until she is better, she's supposed to stay put. So what's the problem? Is the room she's in not suitable?"

"The room's fine, but—"

"Is the house too primitive, the bathroom not clean?"

"No, of course not. But—"

"Is *your* room not okay?"

"Of course it is." Monica raked back her hair with both hands, keeping them clamped around her head as she exclaimed a frustrated, "You're missing the point!"

"Which is?" Zach began spreading mustard on whole wheat.

"We're strangers!"

Zach shook his head. "No we're not. You know my sister. I know your mother."

"But you don't know *me,* nor I *you.* You said you'd take us to Kodiak!"

"And I did. You're on Kodiak Island." Zach layered slices of ham, cheese and tomatoes, closed the sandwich and put it on a plate. "Here, eat. You'll feel better."

Monica dropped her hands and just looked at him. "Why are you doing this?" she finally asked after a tense silence during which she ignored the food he held out. "What do you want from me?"

"Oh, boy." Slow to anger as a rule, but wound pretty tight from the conflicting emotions this woman seemed destined to arouse in him, Zach plunked the plate down in front of her and stepped back. "Some guy really did a number on you, didn't he?" he observed in a soft growl that increased in volume when he added, "But you know something? You're way off base where I'm concerned."

He planted fisted hands on the counter and, leaning toward her, gave her a hard stare. "Ever hear of simple compassion? Huh? Of empathy?"

Unable to look away, to escape the smoldering anger in his eyes, Monica swallowed.

"I felt sorry for the kid," Zach said. "And, hell yes, for you, too! But don't flatter yourself, and insult me, by assuming there's anything more to it than that. There's nothing you have that I want."

Oh, yeah? Grimly, Zach squelched the thought and glared.

Staring back at him in the silence that followed his final salvo, humiliation and shame clogged Monica's throat like dust, choking her. Tears stung the backs of her eyes, but she'd rather die than let them fall. He'd probably regard it as female trickery if she cried. A bid for sympathy after first degrading his kindness—for she did believe now that that had been his only motivation—by assuming ulterior motives.

"I, um—" Her voice was a croak; she swallowed again. "I...don't know what to say. I..." Fed up with herself, she drew a deep breath and squared her shoulders. "I apologize. Okay? Not just for today but for the other night, too. It was kind of you to give me a ride and I'm sorry if I, well...offended you. I..."

She raised her chin a notch and forced her gaze to remain steady though her knees quaked and her stomach was a mess of painful knots. "It's been difficult. Nicole's father..."

"It's okay," Zach said softly when her struggle for words became unbearable for him to watch. The woman clearly had had a rough time of it. "You don't have to explain."

"Th-thanks." Because an errant tear was sneaking down her cheek in spite of her efforts to contain it, Monica looked away.

Zach pretended not to notice. He busied himself with

the food and forced a light tone. "There's milk in the fridge, if you want. Or I could make us some tea...."

Everything considered, lunch had turned out to be a fairly companionable affair. It took only one bite of her sandwich for Monica to realize that she was ravenous. And no wonder, consumed as she'd been with worry over Nicole, she'd been unable to eat neither dinner the previous night nor breakfast that morning.

Zach had been content to let her eat in silence. He had plenty to occupy his own thoughts. Like, for instance, the realization that his outrage at Monica's suggestion of an ulterior motive had partly been fueled by the fact that she hadn't been as off base as he'd tried to make her believe. There was plenty about her that he wanted. Not the least of which was her body. It wouldn't be any kind of hardship to have her in his bed, he ruefully admitted, but that didn't mean he had any intentions of *acting on* those feelings and urges. Especially since...

Walking in back of the house on his way to the hangar about an hour later, he sliced a glare up at the window of the room to which she had retired for a nap.

He was damned near old enough to be her father!

Monica awoke from her nap with a guilty start and was momentarily disoriented. She had slept like the dead. And for the first time in months her slumber had not been haunted by frightening dreams. But... She sat bolt upright and looked around. Where was she? And...Nicole?

Was sick.

Oh, my gosh. In a flash, the day's events rushed back to her. Kodiak. That man, Zach Robinson. Nicky's fever....

With a cry of distress, Monica tossed back the covers and jumped out of bed. She had only removed her jeans and shoes before lying down and quickly slipped into them now. Not bothering with the bathroom she spotted through the half-open door, she simply raked her hair with her fingers and rushed from the room.

Nicole was next door, she recalled. She had checked on her before lying down. But how long ago had that been? It was daylight still, but that didn't mean much. This far north even in late August the days were long.

The door to Nicole's room was open. Monica rushed through it to find Zach at her daughter's bedside. He was holding one of those small plastic cuplets that came with bottles of cough syrup and looked up at Monica's entrance with an expression of exasperated concern.

"She's coughing, but she won't come out from under the covers."

Monica hardly heard him. Her concern was only for her child whose cough, even muffled by the down comforter, was wracking and deep. "Mommy's here, baby." She not very gently shouldered Zach aside. "You should've woken me up."

"You were exhausted."

Zach's exasperation increased as he watched Monica bend over the bed and gently tug on the covers, crooning, "Let me see your face now, sweetheart. There's my girl."

"I'm perfectly capable of giving a child some cough syrup," he grunted.

"Not this child." Monica didn't look up and continued her persuasions. "She's different."

"How?" *Spoiled,* more like, Zach was beginning to think.

"Not now," Monica said in a whisper whose harshness contrasted startlingly with the dulcet tones that immediately followed as the covers slowly moved back. "There's my girl. I can see you now…

"Please leave," she said quietly with a quick glance toward Zach. "Please."

"Fine." Zach set down the medicine and stalked from the room.

Monica spared him a moment's regret, then concentrated on her daughter. "The man's gone now," she said softly, soothingly, urging the covers down. "See?"

Only Nicole's eyes moved as she verified the truth of her mother's words.

"See?" Monica said again and, sliding an arm beneath the fragile little shoulders, gently raised her child up. She took the cough syrup with her free hand. "Here, darling. Yummy. Let's stop this nasty cough…"

She brought the small cup closer, then jumped, startled, when Nicole's hand lashed out and whacked the medicine aside, spilling it.

"Oh, sweetheart…." Momentarily disheartened, Monica pressed her forehead against Nicole's and closed her eyes. Gathering herself, her patience, she nevertheless noted that the child's head felt much cooler. *Thank you for that much, at least.*

She jerked back as another coughing fit wracked Nicole's frail body. Her hands not quite steady, she propped the child up with pillows, then picked the small cup off the floor and refilled a measure of syrup.

Catching her daughter's eye, she smiled reassuringly and took a tiny sip of the medicine. "Hmm, good," she said, licking her lips. "Cherry."

Carefully, she extended the cup toward Nicole. "Your turn," she said. And breathed a sigh of relief when this time the syrup was swallowed.

She stayed with the child until she once again slept. Creeping from the room, she found Zach out in the hall. With one shoulder propped against the wall and his arms folded across his chest, he looked as though he'd been there all along.

Which he had, of course.

As Monica emerged, he pushed himself away from the wall, giving her only a speaking glance before following her through the hall and down the stairs. Halfway to the bottom she sat down. She buried her face in her hands.

Zach sat down next to her. "I'm listening," he said. "If you feel like talking."

"I don't." She shook her head, but didn't lower her hands. "I really don't."

"Okay." Zach figured he had time. He propped his elbows on his knees and rested his chin on his nested hands. As before, her visible distress and vulnerability made him want to gather her close and offer what comfort he could. Platonically, no strings. But he didn't. He simply sat next to her, patient and silent. Minutes passed, their flight punctuated by the steady tick-tock of the massive grandfather clock in the entry below.

At length, Monica took her hands off her face. She copied Zach's position, staring straight ahead, and took a deep breath. "She's not autistic," she said.

Chapter Three

"**S**he's not." Monica's tone was defensive, almost defiant. But when she slowly turned her head until her eyes met Zach's, he saw none of that in their expressive depths.

What he did see as their gazes clung, was pain. Such pain, it squeezed his heart as he watched her eyes darken till they were nearly black. He saw entreaty there, too, in those pain-filled eyes of hers, a silent plea to be believed.

It's important to her, Zach realized with a pang. Why, because no one else had been willing to believe?

"I never thought she was autistic," he quietly assured her. A bit stubborn and spoiled was what he'd thought the child was.

"Why not?" Monica demanded. "It's the first thing others seem to think."

"Others?"

She turned her head away. "Her so-called father, for one."

"Your husband."

Her eyes snapped back to Zach's. "My *ex*-husband," she corrected through clenched teeth.

"Sorry." He meant it, even as a less worthy part of him rejoiced at the vehement correction. It showed that there was definitely no lingering love or regret there. And somehow that mattered even though he knew darned well it shouldn't.

"So why do you care what he thinks?" he asked carefully, so as not to make it seem like he was fishing for details. Which honesty prevailed him to admit he was, in a way. "Since he's out of the picture."

"Because." Monica sighed. She searched Zach's craggy face and wondered if she dared trust him with the truth. She wanted to. She so badly needed to share her burden with somebody. But she was afraid, afraid to trust her instincts, afraid to make a mistake. She decided a half-truth would have to do. She took a deep breath.

"I care," she said, "because Richard Sinclair has a way of popping back *into* the picture whenever he needs something. Like money," she added with a bitter little laugh. "As though I had any left to give."

Oh, boy. Heavy stuff. Zach looked down at his hands, dangling between his spread knees now, and wondered if he really wanted to hear any more. The trouble with confidences was that people tended to regret sharing them, which later on made them want to avoid the person they had shared them with.

He found he didn't want Monica avoiding him. *If* she planned to stay on Kodiak Island.

Unfortunately, it seemed he'd been silent too long. Or, in any case, Monica had read his silence as encouragement. "He bankrupted my business," she was saying in a brittle voice. "Mate-For-You, it was called."

She slanted him a look. "You probably think that's pretty hokey, too."

Ouch. Zach inwardly winced and acknowledged with a sheepish shrug her allusion to his little dig at the Brides for Alaska reader board message two nights ago. Only two nights?

"I guess the name *was* hokey," Monica allowed when Zach remained silent. "But the business was mine and I was proud of it. I started it all by myself with money I inherited from my Grandma Marie not long after Dick and I were married. Dick had his own business then—his family's business, really. Commercial real estate. After his dad retired.

"He drank," Monica said.

"Who? The father?"

"No. Richard."

"Ah."

"Not only that, he gambled."

"I see." He did, indeed, Zach thought, recognizing the pattern. Booze plus gambling equals financial disaster.

It seemed there was more, however.

"He was a violent man when he drank," Monica said. "And later, increasingly, even when he didn't."

Zach stiffened. "He beat you?"

Monica shrugged. She pressed her knuckles against her mouth and didn't look at him.

"And the child?" A surge of rage, all the stronger for its impotence, tightened Zach's voice.

Monica tilted her head back and took a deep breath. "Only once," she said raggedly. "I didn't stick around to give him another chance but…"

Biting down on her lip, she violently shook her head, willing the tears that these days were always threatening, not to fall. When the pressure only increased, she covered her eyes with her hands. "The trouble is, the damage had already been done."

A ragged sob escaped her then. Just one. But the sound of it, and the deep, shuddering breaths with which she fought to regain control, made Zach want to hunt down and beat to a pulp the man who'd done this to her. That, or haul her into his arms and rock her. Soothe her. Comfort her.

Since the latter was at present the only viable option,

Zach put his arm around her shoulders and pulled her close. She didn't resist.

He kissed the top of her head, ashamed of himself because holding her, even like this, felt so darn good. Even right.

Get a grip, man, he chided himself harshly. *With her history, she already thinks most men are animals. Don't give her a reason to add you to that list.*

Ada Gordon chose that moment to bustle into the house. Her sparse eyebrows shot up at the scene on the stairs before her but, heeding Zach's hasty signal for silence, she said nothing. Or, at least not out loud.

"The baby?" she mouthed with exaggerated lip movements that would, under different circumstances, have struck Zach as pretty funny.

As it was he just mutely shook his head and motioned her toward the kitchen.

Monica had heard something, though. She raised her head.

To Zach, gazing down into a face that bore all the marks of emotional exhaustion, she looked achingly vulnerable, causing every one of his protective instincts to jump into action. Nothing and nobody was going to hurt this woman again, he promised himself. Not this woman, and not her little girl. Not as long as he was around.

"Wh-what is it?" Monica asked, alarmed by the feral gleam that had turned Zach's blue eyes to silver.

He dragged up a reassuring smile. "It's nothing. A thought."

"I heard something." Aware, suddenly, that Zach was holding her, Monica pulled back, embarrassed. She scooted away from him, the solidity of him. It had felt much too good. "Someone came in."

"Ada came home." Zach hated letting Monica go, especially since the way she was avoiding his eyes now confirmed what he'd already anticipated—she regretted opening up to him the way she had.

"Ada," Monica said, self-consciously smoothing her hair and looking everywhere but at the man by her side. "She's…"

"My housekeeper. You met her at the airport in Homer."

"Oh, yes. Yes, of course."

"She's in the kitchen." With a sigh, Zach pushed to his feet. He held out a hand. "Come on. I'll ask her to make us some coffee."

"I'd better check on Nicole first." Because she wanted nothing so much as to grab hold of Zach's fingers and let him lead her wherever he would, Monica pretended not to see his extended hand, latching on to the banister, instead. Pulling herself up, she felt old, achy. Her head throbbed and her joints were sore. *Please, God, don't let me have caught Nicole's flu.*

"May I call my mother afterward?" she asked.

"Well, of course." Deciding that some tension-easing and ground-rules-establishing was in order, Zach caught her chin and urged it around with gentle but relentless pressure. "Anything you want," he said when at last her eyes met his. "For as long as you need. Anything at all. No strings."

"Th-thank you," Monica managed to stammer hoarsely past the renewed constriction in her throat. She wished both his eyes and his hand would release her; the man unsettled her on so many levels. He frightened her, but not in the way Richard Sinclair could make her afraid.

This fear was…different. More…emotional. It was scary, but somehow thrillingly electrifying, too.

And altogether too much for her to deal with right now.

She wrenched away and all but fled up the stairs. Zach's hand dropped to his side. With a heavy sigh, he slowly made his way in the other direction.

Ada had shed her coat, put on the apron she was never without in the kitchen, and already had the coffeemaker going. "Where's the woman?" she asked when Zach entered.

"Her name is—"

"I *know* her name," Ada tartly interrupted, plunking a mug of coffee on the table in front of the chair Zach pulled out and straddled. "Didn't I just spend more'n ten hours with her mother?"

"Monica's with her daughter." Zach knew better than to engage in verbal battles with Ada when she got her tail up.

Which she obviously had, because she snapped, "That little girl's name is Nicole."

Zach covered his sigh with a swallow of coffee. "So how was the ferry ride?"

"How d'you think? Choppy'n wet." Ada slapped her own mug down and sat. "That woman is trouble," she announced. "You listen to me and drive her straight home to her people."

Lord, give me patience, Zach thought, and took another sip. "Why?"

"Why?" Ada repeated, visibly offended at having her pronouncement challenged.

Zach decided he might have let her run his private life just a little bit too completely for too long. "That was my question," he said, keeping his tone mild.

Perhaps too mild, since Ada seemed to think that she was still in charge of the situation. "Because," she declared, "she's on the run an' needs a place to hide an' you're the best thing that could've happened to her. I have it straight from the horse's mouth."

"The horse being Carla Romanov, I take it."

"Who else?" Ada stirred sugar into her coffee, then licked the spoon. "The woman's scared witless for her daughter and the child. Said how you were a godsend, flying them over here."

"You thought it was a good idea yourself," Zach reminded her, still mildly.

"Before I knew. Sure." She tested her coffee, blew and, sipping, eyed Zach across the rim of her mug. "Before I caught her plastered against you just now like—"

"That's enough." Surging up off his chair, Zach loomed over her. "I love you like a mother, but I'll thank you to mind your own business in this."

Touched by the old woman's shocked and wounded expression in spite of himself, he softened his stance and his tone. "Doc says the little girl needs to stay put until she's better. Which means she *and* her mother will be our guests. We've always treated guests courteously. Let's not change that now, okay?"

Ada's lips pursed as though she'd just bitten into a lemon. Her nod, when it came, was grudging, at best. But Zach knew she'd honor the commitment, partly for love of him and partly because, as a full-blooded Inuit, being hospitable was in her genes.

"Anyway, I brought some o' their stuff," she mumbled.

"Thanks, Ada. Where is it?"

"Outside. By the front door." She shot him a defiant glare. "Didn't see no point bringing it in if they was gonna be leaving straightaway."

Zach stifled a grin. Trust the old she-devil to get in the last word. Rounding the table, he went and gave her shoulders an affectionate squeeze. "They've been through hell," he murmured.

Only to himself did he add, *And I don't think they or we are out of it yet.*

He knew that if he said that out loud, another inbred Inuit trait would likely supersede the first—fierce loyalty to those they loved. Meaning Ada would move heaven and earth to keep him safe, whether he wanted her to or not.

As he headed for the door to fetch his guests' belongings, he could hear Monica speak to her mother on the phone in the upstairs landing.

"Just a day or two, Mom," she was saying. "Just till Nicky's back on her feet."

Nicky.

His hand on the doorknob, Zach closed his eyes and listened to the echo of that nickname in his head. The face of another little girl, a dark-haired cherub with dimples in her cheeks and eyes as bright as a summer sky, appeared on his mental screen.

Maddy...

Tears stung his lids and, with a muttered oath, Zach wrenched open the door, stepped out and slammed it shut.

That night, every time Monica dragged her aching body out of bed to check on and minister to Nicole, she found Zach in her daughter's room, as well.

"Are you sitting up with her?" she finally asked the third time they met this way. It was three-thirty in the morning. Tired, achy, and barely able to see straight, she felt ill-equipped to deal with having him underfoot.

"Why?" she asked when Zach admitted that, yes, that's what he'd been doing.

Now he shrugged. He didn't really want to explain that he felt compelled to watch over this child because years ago, with another child, his own child, he hadn't watched. And that he had lost her. Confessions like that were for another time, if they were made at all. Someone who looked as ready to keel over as this woman did, had enough on her plate.

"Do you mind?" he asked. "I'm not much of a sleeper at the best of times." Which was true. He rarely slept more than a couple of hours a night, and very lightly, at that. "And she doesn't really notice..."

"Oh, she notices," Monica murmured, gazing down at her sleeping child and marveling, a bit woozily, at the apparent ease with which Nicky now seemed to accept Zach's presence. She bent to straighten the blanket and had to grab the headboard to steady herself as a wave of dizziness made her sway.

"Are you all right?" Zach asked. He rose from the chair, eyes narrowing.

"I...don't know." Monica put a shaky hand over her burning eyes. Her head felt like the slightest movement would splinter it.

"I'm sorry," she murmured. "It's awfully warm in here, don't you think?"

"Well..." Zach looked at her more closely. Not only wasn't it overly warm, it was damned near chilly. He had already tucked a second blanket around the little girl while she slept. He took a step closer and noted that Monica's eyes, clinging to his, were overbright and somewhat out of focus. Simple fatigue? he wondered. Or a fever?

He nudged aside the fingers she was pressing to her forehead and replaced them with his palm. It all but sizzled on contact with her skin. *Uh-oh.*

"Hurts," she murmured, swaying.

"I'll bet." He scooped her up. She was tall, and though slender, her limp form proved quite an armful. "All right, now," Zach huffed. "Let's just get you to bed."

Ignoring Monica's feeble struggles, he carried her to her room, calling, "Ada!" just loud enough to wake the old woman two doors down, but without—he hoped—waking little Nicole.

"You have a kind face," Monica whispered, framing it with hands that were hot and dry as Zach propped his knee on her mattress and gently deposited her there. *"That's* why we're no longer afraid of you, you know. Nicky'n I..."

She seemed to think he knew exactly what she was talking about. Not having a clue, Zach merely nodded and smiled. "I'm glad."

"So'm I." Monica's eyelids were drooping. They really were too heavy, and she really was too tired to hold them up. "My head hurts," she moaned.

"We'll fix you right up here, hon." Ada, comical in a faded wool housecoat and with a hairnet pulled down to her brows, unceremoniously elbowed Zach aside and bent over the bed.

"Fetch me a glass of water," she ordered, and gentling her voice assured Monica, "Ada'll take care o' you, don't you fret."

She made Monica swallow some aspirin, holding her head while helping her drink the water Zach had brought. "There now," she soothed. "You rest and get better."

"Nicky," Monica murmured, her hand moving restlessly on the covers till Ada caught it in both of hers.

"Your baby'll be fine," she crooned. "Zach'n me'll take care of her."

Monica only heard the voice as in a dream. But even so, she somehow sensed things would be all right.

"She's asleep," Ada whispered, gently disentangling herself from Monica's grip.

Together she and Zach crept from the room, leaving the door slightly ajar.

"I thought you didn't like her," Zach said out in the hall.

"Never said I didn't like her." Ada tightened the sash of her robe and drew herself up to her full five-foot-nothing. "Don't trust her not to hurt you, is all."

She studied him, frowning. "You slept yet?"

Zach shook his head. "I'm not tired. You go on back to bed."

She looked at him awhile longer, and Zach could read the worry in her eyes. And the affection. "Mind your heart, Zach," she warned, and, not waiting for a reply, shuffled back to her room.

Zach stayed where he was until her door closed. And counted his blessings.

Which was just as well, because he certainly had none to count over the next couple of hours as he played nursemaid to one sick little girl who, for all she remained stoically silent, most certainly had a mind of her own.

Damn! While that unvoiced oath sizzled on his tongue, Zach struggled to keep his expression kindly and serene as Nicole whacked the cuplet of cough syrup out of his hand for the second time.

All right, he finally thought. Enough of that. Deciding that this was upsetting both of them, and that emotional agitation only made a coughing urge worse, he took a deep breath and set the medication aside.

"Okay," he said. He was sitting on the edge of her mattress and his eyes never left her unblinking regard. "You win. You don't want cough syrup? Fine."

He crossed his legs, settling himself more comfortably. "Sometimes a sip of water helps, too," he said conversationally. He reached for the glass on the nightstand and offered it. At a safe distance. "No? All right."

He put the glass back, reached down to the floor and brought up a copy of *Winnie-The-Pooh.* "In that case I guess I'll just sit here and read awhile to myself. You can listen if you want."

He hadn't expected a response, and didn't get one. He opened the book, leafing through it, as though aimlessly. "Oh, I like this one," he said, admiring the illustrations before holding them up to Nicole with a smile. "It's the one where Christopher Robin and the gang discover the North Pole."

With a chuckle, he returned the book to his lap and began to read. Not really out loud, but loud enough so that she could hear if she cared to listen. He kept his voice low and steady, almost droning. And the next time he looked up, Nicole had fallen asleep. Without any more coughing.

Zach couldn't remember when he'd felt so good about anything. Carefully, so as not to wake her, he eased himself off the bed. He saw the sticky stains on the carpet and decided he'd have Ada clean it up...whenever.

He tiptoed to his rocker in the shadows and sat down. His eyes on the little form on the bed, the book he used to read to Maddy still clutched in his hands, he vowed to stay awake and watch over this child. Just before he fell asleep.

It was the tug on his sleeve that awoke him. *"Maddy?"*

The book was still in his hands and he tossed it aside in his hurry to wake up. He blinked his eyes and shook his head, groaning at the kinks in his back as he straightened in the rocker and groggily looked around.

And saw her then. A tiny form in a too-large shirt, huddling in a heap at his feet. Nicky, he realized with a pang. Not Maddy. She was gazing up at him with unblinking and somber intensity.

Oh, dear God. Rubbing a hand over his bleary eyes, Zach struggled to grasp the situation. *She fell out of bed. No, she'd hardly be sitting here then. Eyes're clear.* Shock had him sitting up straight. *Her eyes are clear!*

Without thinking, he bent and tugged on a lock of her hair. "Hey, punkin, how about that? You're better."

She jerked away from him and scooted out of reach, but otherwise showed no signs of alarm.

Zach, inwardly chiding himself for his impulsive act, returned her solemn gaze. "I'm afraid we're gonna have to make friends, you and I," he said quietly. "Your mommy's sick, you see. Just like you were."

She blinked, but otherwise stayed as she was.

Zach thought, Help. He got to his feet and held out his hand. "Let's go find Ada," he said.

When it became clear that she wasn't about to touch his outstretched hand, he decided his best course was to proceed as though he didn't doubt for a moment that she would follow. He strode out of the room, leaving the door ajar, and walked on down the stairs.

At the kitchen door he turned and was pleased to find her right behind him. "Hungry?" he asked. And, after a moment's hesitation, was rewarded with a cautious nod. "Good girl."

He gave her a smile and ushered her ahead of him into

the kitchen. He pointed to Ada, busy at the stove. "Ada."
He enunciated clearly and slowly as though speaking to
someone with impaired hearing.

This earned him a patient look from two pairs of dark
eyes. Whereupon he fled, leaving these two vastly dispa-
rate, but in their inscrutability, uncannily similar females
to work things out on their own.

A shower and a shave made him feel more like himself.
He wondered how Monica was faring and quietly stepped
up to her bed. She was awake, though barely. To Zach it
seemed a sign of how sick she was, the fact that she didn't
ask about Nicole.

"My head hurts," she complained in a hoarse croak.

Zach, putting his hand to her brow, decided that a call
to Doc Koontz was indicated. "Are you thirsty?" he
asked, not nearly as sure of himself in this sickroom as he
had been in the other one.

"My head," Monica repeated, her voice weak, but filled
now with querulous accusation. "You pushed me…"

Zach realized with alarm that she was delirious.
"Here…" Hoping that a drink of water might help cool
and settle her, he held the glass to her lips, supporting her
head. "Drink…"

"No." She pushed his hand aside. "Don't
want…drink." Her eyes opened wide. They were bright
with fever and locked on his with uncanny lucidity as she
said, very clearly, "That's the problem, don't you see?"

"Monica…" Zach had never felt so out of his depth.
He had to get to the phone and call the doctor. Gently, he
let Monica's head fall back on the pillow. Bending over
her, he smoothed back her hair, an unconscious gesture of
comfort. He stifled the urge to press a kiss on her forehead.

Which was probably just as well, he thought wryly,
when she shoved his hand away with a shudder of revul-
sion and said, "Don't you touch me."

She didn't mean him, Zach reassured himself, not that
he had any business touching her anyway, except in a clin-

ical way, like a nurse. He straightened her covers, his concern escalating as Monica, moaning, tossed her head from side to side on the pillow and whimpered, "Nicky. Oh, please, Dick. Don't. Please, Dick, don't hurt her. Pleeease!"

Zach could barely react fast enough as she suddenly arched off the pillow, her eyes wild, her arms flailing.

"Don't!" she shouted, struggling with Zach who was trying to pin her down, to keep her still. "Let go of me! I'll kill you!"

With staggering force, her fist connected with the side of Zach's face, causing him to rear back as stars danced in his head.

Stunned, he listened as in a voice he barely recognized as hers, Monica vowed, "You hit her again and I swear I'll kill you!"

She was staring right at him and even though Zach knew she wasn't talking to him or even seeing him, the ferocity of her expression sent chills down his spine.

Teeth bared, fists clenched, this was a she-lion protecting her cub. A mother ready to kill to keep her child from harm.

Rooted by the horror that was beginning to make a terrible sort of sense, Zach watched Monica collapse onto the pillow, her lips moving, but not making a sound. His mind went back to the previous day when they'd sat next to each other on the stairs.

And the child? he had asked when she'd told him of her husband's beatings.

Only once, she had said. *But the damage had already been done....*

No. Could it be? Zach stared at Monica who was breathing hard, her fists opening and closing around a handful of bedding. Could a beating by her own father have doomed Nicole to the prison of silence in which she lived?

A murderous rage propelled Zach out of the room. He

would find out, he swore, if it was the last thing he did. And when he had the answer, there was nowhere that miserable excuse for a man could hide to escape Zach's wrath.

He had to take several calming breaths before his fingers were steady enough to stab out Doc Koontz's phone number.

At a time when house calls were no longer part of most doctors' service, it was reassuring to have an old-fashioned medical man like Emmett Koontz at your disposal. He was at Zach's doorstep in less than twenty minutes, bringing with him Carla Romanov.

"Thought you could use an extra pair o' hands," he said to Ada, who was keeping vigil at Monica's bedside.

Keeping Ada in the room with him while he gave Monica a quick once-over, he sent Carla away to check on her granddaughter.

His mini exam of Monica complete, Doc folded his stethoscope and pushed his spectacles up on his forehead. "Flu," he pronounced. "Plenty of fluids, aspirin. Cold compresses..."

He patted Ada's shoulder. "You know the routine."

"She was delirious," Zach insisted when Doc stepped out into the hall. He felt the doctor wasn't taking things seriously enough here. "Doesn't that worry you?"

"Not overly." He peered at the younger man. "How're you holding up with two ailing females in the house?"

Zach shrugged. "The little one's on the mend."

"And the grown-up one will be, too, in a coupl'a days. Carla's with her, but do you want me to look in on the kid?"

Zach shook his head. "Better not. Don't ask how, but Ada managed to get her down for a nap."

"Ada knows what she's about."

"I guess." He wondered what the little one thought about her mother being sick. Given her history, was it possible she imagined that he was in some way to blame?

He pushed the unsettling thought aside, telling himself,

One thing at a time. He had enough worrying him right now without anticipating more problems.

They were down in the entry. Doc, not very subtly, patted his middle. "Haven't had my breakfast, don't you know."

Zach got the hint. He led the way into the kitchen. He wanted to ask Doc some questions, anyway.

Since Ada had her hands full upstairs, he began busying himself with bacon and eggs while the doctor helped himself to coffee. Doing his best to sound nonchalant, Zach said, "Tell me, Doc, what do you know about autism?"

"Autism, eh?" Doc's bushy brows shot up into his receding hairline. He took his time saying anything else as he made himself comfortable at the table. "Can't say's I've had much experience with it."

"But you've read or heard about it, surely?" Zach added another two slices of bacon into the sizzling pan. The smell of it frying was making him hungry, too. It didn't seem right somehow to be hungry when he had so much on his mind, but on the other hand, there was nothing to be gained by starving himself, either. "Like, for instance, could it be brought on by...by some kind of physical trauma like...you know, a beating?"

It sickened him even to form the question; the pictures it conjured up were too abhorrent.

Doc Koontz seemed to think so, too, because his brows beetled into a dark frown as he stared at the man at the stove. "Are we talking hypothetically here or what're you driving at, boy?"

Zach took the pan off the burner and came to the table. He figured breakfast was no longer the uppermost thing on Doc's mind, either. "The little girl," he said. "Nicole. Is she autistic, would you say?"

"Nicole." Doc rubbed a hand over his eyes. "I thought that's what this was about." He dropped his hand and met Zach's troubled gaze. "Sick as she was when I saw her, I couldn't possibly say."

He leaned back, narrowed his eyes. "Now this beating thing, though. What's that all about?"

Zach quickly related the bits Monica had confided, as well as the scene he'd witnessed upstairs. It didn't take long since he didn't know very much.

When he was finished, Doc sighed. "You're taking an awful lot on your shoulders, boy. Are you sure you really want to take this on?"

"Oh, yeah," Zach said with grim determination. "I'm sure."

"Why?"

Zach hesitated, then looked the old man in the eye.

"Because," he said, "I believe this is my chance to redeem myself."

Chapter Four

The old doctor was silent for a while. Zach, too, was still. He was not going to offer any clarification, was not going to elaborate or explain in spite of Doc's doubtlessly sympathetic ear. He knew the doctor wouldn't pry. Mostly because prying simply wasn't done here in what was popularly known as America's Last Frontier where many came to leave their past behind. Doc would respect a man's right to privacy.

"True autism," Doc said at length, just as though he were merely continuing an existing conversation, "is, to the best of our knowledge, a mental disorder the affected child develops sometimes before the age of three. It's relatively rare in girls. Four times as common in boys, as a matter of fact. Can it be caused by...physical abuse?"

He spread his hands. "Who knows? All o' that—cause, cure and what-have-you—is still being studied. Some say genetics play a role. Others think some sort of degenerative nerve disease or some such is at the root of it. O'course..."

He yanked his spectacles off his forehead and polished them with his handkerchief, remarking, "That bacon smells good enough to eat, Zach,'' before getting back to his original thought. ''Kids *will* respond to violence in the home in whatever way they can best cope, you know.''

''Like, for instance?'' Zach prompted, putting the frypan back on the burner to get on with Doc's breakfast. His own appetite had fled.

''Withdrawal.'' Satisfied that his glasses were clean, Doc positioned them on his nose and took a sip of his coffee. Grunting, ''Stuff's cold,'' he got to his feet and tossed it out in the sink. ''Complete emotional withdrawal.''

''But that's what autism is.''

''Nope.'' Doc refilled his cup, testing it before resuming his seat. ''Withdrawal is voluntary. Autism is not. Withdrawal can be reversed—and please note that I say *can*, as in it's possible. I'm not saying it's probable.''

''But you think that Nicole...'' Eggs forgotten, Zach loomed over Doc across the table. A surge of excitement made his heart beat faster. He recalled the gleam he thought he'd seen in Nicky's eyes the second time she'd smacked away the cough syrup. Could it be possible that behind that stoic, self-protective silence lurked a normal little girl just waiting for someone to release her?

''Now really, Zach.'' Doc Koontz eyed Zach with more than a hint of exasperation. ''How can I think anything until I've had a chance to look at the girl when she's awake?''

It took three more days before Monica was well enough to get out of bed. Three days in which Carla Romanov became yet another guest at Windemeer for the simple reason that she had become—once again—the only person Nicole would tolerate near her. And even at that, she stayed huddled in the corner of her room, clutching her woolly stuffed rabbit, and keeping the rest of the world at bay with her unblinking regard.

When the doctor came in, she promptly turned around

to face the wall. No amount of coaxing from her grandmother could budge her.

Her reaction to Zach's or Ada's presence was less dra-
matic in that she didn't present them with her back. But
she also gave no sign of recognition such as she did with
Carla, whom she followed with her eyes. And whom she
would look at when spoken to, and also permitted to wash,
dress and feed her. Though she ate alarmingly little.

Zach's interlude with her in the night, and Ada's that
following morning, might never have taken place. Still,
Zach refused to be daunted. He made it a point to spend
several hours a day just sitting in the rocking chair in Nicole's room, either reading to her or simply returning her
stare with one of kindness and reassurance.

He was increasingly sure the child could be reached especially when, on the third day, he winked at her. And she
blinked.

That the child was pining for her mother was obvious
even without tears or a tantrum. Nicky's attachment to that
one particular corner of the room was ample indication to
Zach of how lost she must be feeling. It seemed to him
that by huddling there, she had shrunk her world to a man-
ageable dimension. And since the situation was, by the
very nature of Monica's illness, only temporary, he saw
no reason to try to coax the child away from where she
felt safe.

Still, everyone heaved a sigh of relief when the doctor
pronounced Monica well enough to be Mommy again.

Zach insisted he be the one to escort Nicole next door.
To do so, he came to her room first thing in the morning.
Carla had just taken the little girl to the bathroom, but she
was still dressed in the little granny nightgown that even
covered her toes.

Her fine reddish hair had been brushed to a shine and
hung in gentle curls past her shoulders. Her eyes were
fixed on the doorway through which, after knocking, Zach
entered the room.

His own gaze went to Carla's. Had his knock drawn Nicole's attention?

Carla gave no indication she understood his silent query and, of course, there was no way he'd ask out loud. He had become convinced, as he knew Monica to be, that Nicole perfectly understood every word that was spoken.

More, he had become convinced that if she wanted to, Nicole could speak. He had said as much to Doc Koontz and had wondered aloud just how he might trick or persuade Nicole to use her voice.

"Incentives," the old man had replied. "Present her with something she wants badly enough to ask for."

Wishing Nicole a good morning now, Zach wondered what in the world might entice this little girl to speak. Wouldn't it be something if she said *Mommy* when they went to see Monica in a moment or two.

"You ready to see *Mommy?*" he asked, emphasizing the word as he hunkered down in front of the child so as to be at eye level. He took heart from the fact that she did not scoot to her corner. She did back up a few steps, though, until her back was against her grandmother's legs.

Zach pretended not to notice the maneuver. And he also didn't alter his normal voice and demeanor the way Ada tended to do. She seemed to think she had to talk all gooey and sweet and keep a smile on her face when dealing with the child no matter how often Zach or Doc had made it clear Nicole was not an invalid.

"Poor little lamb," she'd say, adding with scornful disdain, "What do you men know about it, anyway?"

"Mommy's been sick," he said, watching Carla brush the top half of Nicole's hair into a ponytail and tie it with a ribbon. The little girl's deep brown eyes were huge beneath the fringe of her bangs. Huge, but surely not empty.

Zach looked into them, deeply, searchingly. "You remember that Mommy's been sick, don't you, sweetheart?" he asked quietly, and felt vastly encouraged by the flicker of response he thought he saw. "That's why she hasn't been with you. That's why Grandma here, and Ada, and I—'' he touched his chest ''—*Zach*, have been taking care of you these past coupl'a days.

"And Rabbit, too, of course," he added, pleased that Nicole didn't flinch when he playfully poked the rabbit's chest.

"C'mon." He rose, and held out his hand. "Let's go see if *Mommy*'s awake."

He didn't really expect her to take his hand, and she didn't. In fact, she didn't move, period. Zach walked to the door, deciding to leave it to Carla to coax her to follow. He forced himself not to look back as he stepped into the hall. He purposely dawdled as he covered the short distance between rooms, knocked and, at Monica's call, opened the door.

It wasn't until, when he stuck his head inside and saw Monica's eyes fly from his to someplace closer to the floor that he realized Nicole had caught up with him like the silent little shadow she was.

No longer a shadow, though, as Monica, with a glad cry, opened her arms and Nicole sped past Zach's legs and launched herself onto the bed.

Watching her burrow into her mother while desperate sounds like rusty sobs sounded from deep in her throat, Zach felt his own throat grow painfully tight.

Monica was openly weeping as she rocked Nicole. "My baby, my baby," she crooned, covering her child's face with kisses.

Nicky clung tightly to her mother, but the eyes she turned to Zach, huge pools the color of darkest chocolate beneath the now disheveled fringe of bangs, were dry. And she didn't speak.

After Nicole had been put to bed the next evening, they had a conference in the kitchen—Zach, Monica, Carla and the doctor. It had been precipitated by Carla Romanov's announcement that it was time Monica and Nicole came to her house to stay.

Zach was against the idea for a variety of reasons, not all of which he was proud of or cared to examine too closely. Like, for instance, how good it felt to have a "family" to care about and be involved with. Or how much it pleasured him to simply look at Monica; to watch her interact with her child, and to fantasize about Monica being his. Belonging to him, and desiring him as he desired her. Intensely. Carnally.

But the overriding reason he wanted to keep them at Windemeer truly was altruistic. He simply didn't think Nicole's well-being would be best served by yet another move to yet another strange house.

To his relief, Doc Koontz was firmly allied with him on that score. "This child has undergone a tremendous amount of trauma in the past couple of weeks," he declared, addressing Monica. "And I'm not even taking into account what all might've gone on before you brought her to Alaska."

He held up a hand when Monica drew breath to speak. "We don't need to go into any particulars here and now," he said. "Any five-year-old would have trouble adjusting to the string of changes your little one's been subjected to, but especially one who is as shy and…withdrawn as your little girl.

"For whatever reason." He forestalled another attempt by Monica to speak. "And to whatever extent. I only want to make clear that I'm in perfect agreement with Zach in that, for the time being, at least, I think you and the child should stay here. She's just becoming familiar. Why, I saw her outside with you earlier and she stopped to pat that mangy old cat Ada keeps around."

Monica nodded. "She did. I was pretty astounded, myself."

Doc turned to Carla, who looked troubled. "Correct me

if I'm wrong, Mrs. Romanov, but the child has never met your husband, has she?''

"No, she hasn't. But Pete's great with kids,'' Carla hastened to add. "He's got several grandkids from his first marriage and—''

"You know that isn't the issue," Doc gently interrupted. "He could be Santa Claus himself and Nicole would still be frightened.''

"Lots o' kids are scared of Santa Claus," Ada grunted in the background.

Doc grinned at her. "Right. Maybe that wasn't such a good example. But you get my meaning," he said to Carla, turning serious again. "Nicole doesn't need to meet any more strangers right now.''

"And I've got plenty of room for guests," Zach put in.

Which prompted Ada to sourly inject, "Yeah, but they're gen'rally the paying kind. In summer.''

Zach shot her a glare that promised he'd have a word with her later. He knew it was concern for his emotional well-being that prompted Ada's ill-mannered comments, though, to her credit, she was kindness itself in her dealings with the child. Still, enough was enough.

In fact, more than enough, he thought angrily when Monica spoke up with a quiet, "It goes without saying that I'll pay for room and board.''

"Absolutely not!" Zach barked, not sure who exasperated him more, his guest or his housekeeper. "We rent rooms in the summer to clients who charter me and my planes for hunting and fishing trips. This is something else entirely and I don't want to hear another word about it!''

Monica thought it best to let the matter go for the moment, but had no intention of being a freeloader. If not with Zach, then she'd work something out with Ada who, no doubt, resented the extra burden she had to shoulder with guests in the house. She, Monica, could certainly help with the housework while she figured out how best to proceed from here.

It went without saying that staying at Windemeer was, at best, a temporary solution. And perhaps even moving in with her mother and stepfather was not such a hot idea. Because with all the goodwill in the world, nobody could put up with houseguests on any kind of permanent basis.

She had to make a home, a home of their own, for herself and her child. And soon. Very soon.

"Just one more move, my sweet," she whispered later that night, bending over the sleeping child and pressing a soft kiss onto the smooth forehead behind which slumbered so many secrets. "Just one more...."

"One more...*what?*" Zach asked quietly, startling her nonetheless as she crept from her daughter's room.

Monica shook her head. No way was she going to tell him her plans because she knew Zach would try to talk her out of them. Though Lord knew why.

She went down the stairs and out onto the porch that wrapped around the entire house. It, like the house itself, had been built of sturdy timbers and stained a deep brown. The color of Nicole's eyes, she thought, draping an arm around one of the supports. She was aware that Zach had followed her outside, though not because she'd heard his footsteps. She seemed to have acquired some special sort of antenna where he was concerned. And it bothered her that this was so. She told herself that—for crying out loud!—he wasn't even good-looking. That he was merely...well—all man.

Which, given her history, should be enough in itself to send her running like the wind in any direction but his.

So why was it, she kept asking herself, that being close to him rather than getting away was what she dreamed about at night? Idiocy, that's what.

A board creaked as Zach moved toward her, but Monica didn't speak. And Zach, too, kept silent.

Though it was well past nine o'clock, the sun was just setting. Monica concentrated on admiring the richness of color in the evening sky and the long, orange and gold rays gilding the waters of Shelikof Straight. The air was chilly with a hint of dampness, but not cold.

Hugging herself even though she knew the goose bumps on her arms had less to do with the little breeze that barely stirred the grass than an awareness of Zach's bulky presence just behind her, Monica turned her gaze to the left, away from the water to the runway on which Zach had landed his plane. Beyond that a ways, she saw trees. Lots of trees.

"How far does your land go?" she asked when the silence between them began to take on an unsettling life of its own.

"Pretty much all the way into town," Zach replied after first clearing his throat. It had gone dry simply from standing close enough to smell Monica's sweet, womanly scent.

She half turned to look at him across her shoulder. "How far is town?"

Catching her gaze and holding it, Zach shrugged. "Ten, twelve miles."

"Which way?" Annoyed by the breathlessness of her voice, Monica forced her eyes frontward again.

Zach came to stand next to her and pointed. Looking in the direction he indicated, Monica still saw nothing but trees.

"Why did you bring us here?" she asked. "Instead of to town?" She knew full well that he wouldn't like what she was about to say. Which was precisely the reason she wanted to say it—dealing with him on an adversarial basis was easier than talking to him as a friend. "If you had taken us straight to my mother's, I wouldn't now need to impose…"

"You're not imposing," Zach growled. "And I brought you here for no other reason than that it would've been a damned nuisance to fly the plane back here from the other airport."

Not strictly the truth, but as good a reason as he was going to offer. "Besides, your mother wasn't there."

"Pete was."

"Nicole doesn't know Pete."

"She didn't know you then, either."

"Maybe not, but she'd already been through the trauma of first meetings, so the worst was over."

Monica turned to face him, her back stiff and straight against the pillar. "There's no way you're going to let me win this argument, is there?"

"I didn't know this was an argument."

She tilted her head back and forced herself to meet his silver-blue gaze. "Why are you doing this? Can you tell me?"

Zach's reply wasn't any more satisfactory than it had been the first time she'd asked him that question. He shook his head. "No."

When Monica simply continued to gaze at him in silence, he added, "Not yet," thinking it was one thing to talk of self-redemption to Doc Koontz, but quite another to bare his soul to this woman who, though she didn't know it, already had too much influence on his emotional equilibrium. "And maybe never. But don't worry, it's not because I expect anything back from you in return."

"I suppose that's reassuring," Monica murmured with a trace of bitterness. She was terribly tired, suddenly, and feeling way too vulnerable to remain out here with Zach in the gathering dusk. She pushed away from the pillar. "Since I have nothing to give."

"Now that's where you're wrong." Zach put out his arm and barred her way when she tried to step past him.

Startled, and instantly wary, her gaze snapped to his. But she stayed, even when Zach dropped his hand and, his voice husky, said, "You've got plenty, Monica. A wealth of qualities any woman would envy and every man desire."

Momentarily mesmerized by the light in Zach's eyes and the sweetness of his words, Monica's throat worked at a lump of emotion. But then she recalled herself and vehemently shook her head. "Not every man. Not Richard…"

"He's a fool."

"And, by your own admission, not you." She moved past him to the door, then looked back. "Remember?"

Zach nodded. Yeah, he remembered. But out loud he said, "If you really believe I meant that, then you're a fool, too."

Rebecca called the next day.

Zach was in his office which was located at the other end of his property in what, at first glance, looked like a garage. He was catching up on accumulated mail. With everything that had gone on this past week, he hadn't even set foot in the place, though Ruth Mencken, his part-time secretary, obviously had. The mail had been sorted and neatly stacked on his desk according to importance.

Ruth was meticulous, though slowing down and fed up with Kodiak's damp and cold winters. Several weeks ago she had announced her intention to be permanently basking in Florida sunshine come mid-September or, at the latest, by October first.

Out of touch with what day it was, Zach checked the calendar, which had been flipped to September. Today was Tuesday, it seemed. September first. Ruth had marked it in red with the message: Start Thinking Replacements, Boss!

Zach's lip curled. Cute. He was reaching for the phone to call up the Kodiak *Mirror* to place an ad when it rang. "Robinson."

"I guess it's Ruth's day off." Becky generally launched into telephone conversations without the customary opening lines. At least, when she called her brother she did.

"Ah, Rebecca," Zach responded dryly and, as though she *had* observed the amenities, added, "I'm pretty good, thanks. How about yourself?"

"Wondering why I'm even speaking to you," Becky

said tartly. "Notice it took me a while to decide whether I would or not."

"Has it been a while?" Zach tut-tutted. "How time flies."

"Sure, go ahead. Be a smart aleck. You're not the one who had to cope with extra women on her hands that Friday night and Saturday."

"You didn't really expect me to show up again Saturday, did you?" Figuring he might as well be comfortable while being chewed out, Zach kicked back and put his feet on his desk. "You must've realized I'd taken all I could Friday night."

"Yeah, yeah," Becky muttered, audibly mellowing. "I forgot about how sensitive you are. Ah, well..." She sighed. "It wouldn't have been so bad if Monica Griffith hadn't had to abandon me, too."

At the mention of Monica's name, Zach tensed. He yanked his feet off the desk and let his chair snap forward.

"A sick child or something," Becky was saying. "I don't know. Poor woman hasn't been herself for quite some time. You remember her, don't you? The blonde?"

"Sure, I remember." Zach couldn't have said why he was being cagey. Why he didn't just tell his sister where Monica was.

"Well, it's the funniest thing," Rebecca said. "Some guy comes barging into my office today, demanding to know where she is."

Zach's fingers gripped the phone more tightly. "What did you tell him?"

"Why, the truth, what else? I haven't a clue where she's got to."

"Did he believe you?"

"Why wouldn't he? It's the truth."

"What'd he look like?"

"I don't know—tallish, balding. Flashy dresser, but— Wait a minute!"

Just like that, Becky's tone of desultory complaint

changed to one of demand. "What's going on here, brother, dear? Why the fifth degree all of a sudden? What aren't you telling me?"

Zach rubbed his brow with a sigh. He knew better than to try to play dumb. Once her suspicions were aroused, Rebecca was like a bloodhound on the scent—relentless. Besides, if there was one person in the world he completely trusted, his sister was it.

"She's here," he said. Any other time he would have been amused by the total silence that followed his words. Rendering Rebecca Sanders speechless was no mean accomplishment. "She and the little girl," he added.

"The little girl," Rebecca repeated flatly.

"Her daughter." Zach pinched the bridge of his nose. "Nicole." As concisely as he could, he filled his sister in, ending with a somber, "I just hope that wasn't the husband on her trail."

"How could it be?" Becky demanded. "Why would he be?"

"I don't know." Zach got to his feet. "But I guess it behooves me to try to find out."

Chapter Five

It wasn't easy for Zach to catch Monica alone. Nicky, when not asleep, was almost constantly by her mother's side now that Carla had returned to her own home. And Monica, after their tête-à-tête the other evening, seemed to make it a point not to be caught in his company by herself.

Zach wished he'd damned well kept his mouth shut that night. He was too old, she was too hurt, and they both lugged around more baggage than an airport skycap. He had no business getting personal with her. Coming on to her. None.

The weather was fine today, sunny and mild. Ada told Zach, when he grimly inquired into their guests' whereabouts, that Monica had taken the little girl out for some exploring around the grounds. Inwardly applauding the move since expanding the child's world could only be beneficial if done in a careful, systematic fashion, Zach went in search of them.

He didn't even bother looking in the hangar which was the domain of Roger Creswell, the thirty-five-year-old Australian bush pilot and airplane mechanic who'd wan-dered into Zach's charter operation a couple of years ago. The man was a marvel with anything that flew, including Zach's aging HUEY and the temperamental Aerobat that Zach still liked to take up once in a while for a loop-the-loop or hammerhead stall. Roger kept them, as well as the two Cessnas—one of them a float plane—in prime condition. He also spelled Zach as pilot for the various hunting or fishing charters they ran in the summer.

"Roge" was an amiable sort who, if he had any secrets, hadn't offered to divulge them. Nor had Zach, with more than his share of secrets himself, bothered to ask. He didn't care what, if anything, the man might have left behind in his native Queensland—if that truly was the Australian state from which he hailed—as long as he did his job in a dedicated and honest fashion.

Walking past it after Deke McBride—his other mechanic—told Zach he'd seen the woman and child head for the north pasture where a few head of Angus grazed, Zelda, Mitch's highly pregnant malamute bitch, waddled up for her customary scratch behind the ear. Zeus, her mate, watched from the stoop by the door with blue-eyed disdain for such mollycoddling.

"Not long now, huh, old girl," Zach muttered, digging his fingers deep into the big dog's luxuriant silver-and-black coat as he scratched so as to give her the most pleasure. "And, hey, maybe one o' your pups just might be able to make a little girl smile...."

An idea worth keeping in mind, Zach thought. Inhaling deeply, savoring the invigorating mix of salty air, dew-wet grass and hemlock as he walked toward the pasture, he decided he didn't walk his land often enough. You missed out on the smells when you drove an A.T.V., even if it did get you where you were going a heck of a lot faster than walking.

Speed. Speed and crowds were among the things he'd come here to Kodiak to get away from. And yet, more and more, it seemed the outside world was catching up with

him again. Hell, he'd even taken on a couple of legal cases
this past year. Nothing earthshaking, an estate dispute and
some property line hassles, but he'd nevertheless gone
back on a promise he'd made—namely to keep himself
out of the public eye as completely as he could.

*And that includes letting yourself be bamboozled into
squiring so-called Brides For Alaska for your bossy old
sister.*

Except, if he'd done as he'd wanted, if he'd turned
Becky down, he wouldn't have met Monica, would he?
And Nicole. Little Nicky who, if not a substitute for his
own little girl, just might be the key to his...well, salvation
sounded too grandiose, but self-forgiveness might do. He
craved an end to *if only.* And peace. He longed for peace.

Zach compressed his lips as if by parting them he'd let
escape the pain he felt he didn't yet deserve to let go. He
squinted into the distance and noted that Monica had spotted him. She was squatting, talking to Nicky, gesturing
toward him, preparing the little girl for his approach. He
was heartened when Nicole turned to face him, hugging
her woolly rabbit with both arms, but without any outward
sign of alarm.

"Hi, there, Nick," Zach greeted her, and really felt good
when she didn't flinch as he playfully tugged on one of
her braids.

Hoping for a smile even though he knew none would
likely be offered, he then clapped his palm to his head,
and said, "What's the matter with me, calling you Nick?
Nick's a boy's name! And anyone can see that you, little
lady—" He hunkered down and touched a finger to the
tip of her tilted little nose. "Are one cute little girl."

Returning her solemn stare, he felt his throat close up.
Wishing with all his might that he could scoop her up and
hug her to his heart and make the hurt go away, he gave
her a crooked little smile. It took a lot of effort, and he
quickly straightened to hide his real emotions.

Another pair of huge somber eyes met his then. Eyes

more hazel than chocolate and vastly more expressive. Which didn't make them any easier to deal with. Because they stirred him, too, in different though no less powerful ways.

"It's okay for us to be out here, isn't it?" Monica asked a little anxiously. "It's such a pretty day and... We've been enjoying the cows," she added, disconcerted by Zach's steady regard. And by the way her foolish heart had leaped at the sight of him.

"They wouldn't like you calling them that," Zach said, nodding toward the half dozen black beasts grazing and munching in the field.

"They wouldn't?" Reacting to the gleam of humor in Zach's eyes, Monica bent to her daughter and in a stage whisper said, "They look like *cows* to us, don't they, sweet?"

She felt like shouting, *See? She understands!* when Nicky first turned her eyes to the cattle and then back up to her. Her own eyes flew to Zach's to see if he shared her conviction, and they misted when he smilingly nodded his head.

Their gazes locked for a moment, a dizzying moment during which all the blood seemed to leave Monica's head and rush to her heart. She wanted to look away, but couldn't quite seem to will herself to do so. There was so much...light kindling in the eyes that so effortlessly held her own, so much...*fire*...

A tug at her sleeve broke the spell, drawing her gaze back down to her daughter who raised one hand and pointed. Monica immediately dropped down on one knee and looked beyond the pointing little finger.

"Cows," she said approvingly.

"Steers," Zach dryly corrected from the other side of the child.

Both of them were more than a little surprised when Nicole vehemently shook her head and pointed again, her little finger stabbing the air. To see Nicky display even this degree of animation was exhilarating.

It prompted the adults to make a real effort to see what she was trying to point out to them. Zach bent to her level, narrowing his eyes. And...there!

"A rabbit!" Monica exclaimed. "Oh, Nicky!"

"Sonovagun." Zach shook his head at the sight of a gray cottontail perched on its hind legs, ears up in an attitude of alertness. Nose twitching.

"A bunny rabbit," Monica repeated, and was almost delirious with joy when Nicole held out her own worn and woolly rabbit, looking first at Zach and then her mother as if for confirmation.

Monica gave it in a choked voice. "Yes, darling. A bunny, just like yours."

Zach had to turn away to keep his own emotions from getting the better of him. He could well imagine what Monica was feeling. Because each tiny, minuscule sign of progress in the child represented a victory. Over her husband, over adversity, over whatever demons little Nicky was battling. He was only glad that he was, in whatever small way, able to contribute to her victory.

Monica, momentarily undone, hugged Nicky with her eyes squeezed shut against the sting of grateful tears. "I knew it," she whispered. "Oh, thank God. I knew it."

Needing to convey to her that he shared her elation, Zach bent to gently squeeze her shoulder. To his surprise, Monica turned her head and pressed a fervent kiss on the back of his hand.

Zach yanked it back. *What the hell?* He stared at Monica without comprehension.

"Thank you," she said, her voice uneven. "For giving us this." Her eyes brimmed as she got to her feet and made a sweeping motion with her hand that encompassed the land, the trees, the cattle. The calm. "This is what we needed. And without you it would never have been possible."

"Well." Uneasy with all this emotion, Zach looked away, clearing his throat. He felt Monica's impulsive kiss like a brand on the back of his hand. It occurred to him, as those irreverent kinds of thoughts always tended to at inappropriate moments, that if he were young again, he probably wouldn't want to wash that hand for at least a week. "I, uh... I'm just glad to be able to help, that's all."

"Yes, well, I... I appreciate it."

Self-conscious suddenly, Monica took Nicole's hand and slowly started walking back toward the house.

When Zach fell into step beside her, she asked, "Did you, uh, just happen to come out here or were you, er, looking for us?"

"Looking for you." Shoving both hands into the pockets of his denims, Zach wondered how to proceed. Loathe to drag a dark cloud across Monica's sunny day, he squinted out over the Strait as if for inspiration.

"Becky called," he finally said, knowing that in itself explained exactly nothing.

"Oh." Monica felt bad about having left the other woman in the lurch. Why, she hadn't even spoken to Rebecca since her hasty departure from the reception. First Nicky's and then her own illness had driven all other concerns completely out of mind. "Did she say how the Brides thing went?"

"It went okay." Zach kicked at a pebble. "She's ticked at me for not showing up on Saturday for more escort duty."

"Oh? And why didn't you?"

Zach's sideways glance was a silent reprimand. "One evening with those barracudas was all I could take."

"Barracudas?" Monica tut-tutted. "Shame on you. Are you so secure and self-satisfied in your bachelor existence you can't dredge up some sympathy for people who are lonely?"

"Sure I can." Zach sent another pebble flying, and shared a pleased grin with Monica when Nicky kicked one, too. "But from a distance," he added, finishing his answer to Monica's question. "And I'm far from secure and self-satisfied, as you put it."

"Well, maybe I didn't put it very well." Monica was sensitive enough to pick up on Zach's slightly injured tone. "And I certainly didn't mean it in a derogatory way. But the fact is that you've chosen to make your life in this rather remote part of the world, and you've chosen to do it alone. Am I right?"

"As far as it goes, yes, you're right."

"As far as it goes." Monica pursed her lips. "So what did I miss?"

"Just about everything that isn't pat and superficial," Zach said very seriously. "Things, people, are rarely what they seem on the surface. Take you, for instance—"

"We were talking about *you*," Monica interrupted, much preferring to keep it that way. "I overheard at the party that twenty years ago you used to be a basketball star. A celebrity, even. Sorry I didn't recognize you...."

"I'm glad you didn't. The guy I was then isn't someone I'm particularly proud of. I've worked very hard to leave him behind."

"I guess it'd be nosy of me to ask why you felt you needed to."

"Yeah, I guess it would."

"Will you tell me anyway?"

"Only if you tell me something first."

"Like what?" Even as she asked, a frisson of alarm shivered down Monica's back. Was it possible that Zach knew she hadn't been completely open with him about her dealings with Richard? How? Unless her mother...

But no, Carla would never involve a relative stranger in family problems. She wasn't even very happy about Monica's continued stay here at Windemeer.

Telling herself to quit being paranoid, Monica stopped walking when Nicole let go of her hand. She watched as the child bent to pick some daisies.

"Look at her," she said softly but vehemently. "And don't tell me that child is in any way retarded."

"Who the heck says she is?" Zach decided that a shift in the conversational direction might be for the best, after all. Since he was in no way anxious to spill his guts about his past, maybe it wasn't fair to expect Monica to. "Her father?"

"Why do you say that?" Monica asked, and the expression of wariness in her eyes reminded Zach that there were many ways other than verbal in which people provided answers.

But though he was convinced now that there was more to her attitude than simple antipathy for a troublesome ex, he merely shrugged. "You once told me he considers her autistic. Remember?"

"Oh, yes. I do remember, now that you mention it." Some of the tension left her shoulders as Monica recalled the interlude on the stairs. But the headache that had sprung up intensified. She rubbed her brow. "But surely you've seen enough for yourself by now to agree with me that she isn't."

"Oh, absolutely," he said, watching Nicole and marveling at her ability to pick flowers with both hands and not drop her rabbit. "I talked to Doc Koontz about it, you know. About autism. Its causes, prognosis, stuff like that."

"And?" Monica prompted eagerly when he just watched Nicole in silence awhile.

Zach turned his head and was touched by the anxiety in her eyes. "Your eyes are the color of amber right now," he said softly, and put a finger to her lips when she drew a breath to protest. "Relax. It's not a come-on, merely an observation of fact."

He tucked a windblown wisp of hair behind her ear, letting his finger linger for just an instant before drawing his hand away. "Doc shares your feelings. He thinks her withdrawal is voluntary, which autism never is. He thinks, suspects, that in Nicky's case a kind of defense mechanism triggered it, that it's a way for her to cope with…whatever.

"He also thinks that while it won't be easy to reverse the condition, it can be done, if she's given some strong incentives. Right now, as things stand, life's not so bad from Nicky's perspective and she might not see any reason to change. She has you at her beck and call, she's loved, fed, clothed.…"

"Well, of *course,* she is. And she's thriving, isn't she? Are you suggesting I stop all that?"

"Lord, no."

"But you said that Doc said…"

"That it might take something more, maybe even a shock of some kind, to bring her back completely. That's all. In the meantime, what you've *been* doing is great. Like I said earlier, even I can see progress. And it's bound to get better, slow but sure."

"Slow but sure." Monica bit her lip, her voice heavy. "Do you know how hard it is for me to be patient? If only…" She checked herself with a shake of the head.

All too familiar himself with *if only,* Zach found himself wishing there were something he could say to assure her that anything was possible. He doubted he could make it sound convincing, though, since he didn't really quite believe it himself.

"If only…*what?*" he coaxed.

Monica looked at him, saw how honest caring was creasing his rumpled face. She looked into his eyes, as blue as the waters of the Strait were today with that bright sun up above. And she saw caring there, too.

As well as other things, unnerving things. Man-woman things that both excited and frightened her, if she were to indulge herself by dwelling on them. Which she wouldn't. Couldn't. Certainly not right now. And, if she were smart, not at any other time, either.

"Why are you so good to me?" she whispered with a little catch in her voice. "To us?"

Zach waved the question away, almost angrily. She seemed to think of him as some kind of guardian angel whose motives were pure. When the truth was, there was a whole lot ulterior to his motives. A whole lot that was less than strictly altruistic.

"You said *if only* as though having whatever you're wishing come true would make you and Nicky a whole lot happier. So what is it? Anything I can help with?"

"You're doing more than your share already."

Since Zach didn't think giving someone a few days of sanctuary was worth all that much in the greater scheme of things, he made no reply. He shifted his attention to Nicole. She was tossing grass through the wires of the pasture fence, ripping out more and tossing that, too. But not randomly, he noted.

"Hey, look…" He gave Monica a nudge. "She's feeding the steers."

"Told you she's smart," Monica said, her preoccupation with Zach and his motives instantly shunted aside by this minor little victory. She pressed her nested hands to her lips to contain a wistful sigh. "Now if we could only get her to talk…"

Maybe she's mute, Zach thought, but hadn't the heart to suggest such a thing out loud. "Has she ever?" he asked instead. "Talked, I mean?"

"Oh, yes. When she was smaller… Baby words. You know, Mama, Dada, puppy, ball. Those kinds of things." Sadness made Monica's shoulders droop. "What I'd give to hear her call my name…"

"You will," Zach said with more conviction than he felt. But when Nicole actually ran up and offered them each a flower, he shared Monica's delight.

Nicole's daisies graced the dinner table that night. Ada had found a little vase for them and Nicky had watched her mother fill it with water and put the daisies in.

"Pretty flowers," Monica said distinctly. She felt that

if she enunciated clearly, Nicole would better be able to pronounce the words when the time was right for her to speak. She was convinced that the vocabulary was there in her child's little brain. It was there and it was growing and in time she would articulate. And in the meantime, Monica refused to even entertain the possibility of being wrong.

The mood over dinner was upbeat. For the first time since she couldn't remember when, Monica allowed herself to relax. Just a little. They were safe here. They were far from anywhere danger might lurk and they could take some time to regroup. And to plan.

"Hey," Zach said, sounding impressed, and drawing Monica back to the here and now. "Look who ate up all her chicken and dumplings..."

Narrowing his eyes, he ducked his head and squinted at Nicky's rabbit, secure in the crook of her left arm. "You didn't by any chance help her, did you, Rabbit?"

Getting into the game, Monica, sitting on Nicky's other side, snuck out a hand and wiggled the rabbit's head from side to side.

"No, I didn't," she said in a squeaky little voice that drew a wide-eyed stare from her little girl.

"Are you sure?" Zach growled. "Let me feel." He poked the rabbit's tummy. "Well, I'll be! It's empty, all right."

He looked at Monica. "What do you think, should I check Nicky's tummy, too?"

Monica exchanged a glance with her daughter. Something in the child's eye—an uncertainty she sensed more than saw—told her it would be best if *she* did the checking for now. This kind of play, this kind of teasing was, after all, something new for her child.

"I'd better do it," she said importantly. "Because I am the mommy and Mommies know just where to check."

Still speaking, she quickly reached out and tickled Nicole's free side and ribs. "I feel chicken," she laughed. "Here, and here. And all the way over...here..."

She could have wept for joy when, with a smothered little sound that might almost have been a giggle, Nicky hugged her arms around herself and scrunched in a self-protective little curl.

"And did you feel a hole for dessert somewhere in there?" Zach queried. "It's chocolate ice cream, isn't it, Ada?"

Over by the sink, Ada dabbed at her eyes with an edge of her apron while muttering, "Darned foolishness anyway, grown people playin' around at the table."

After Nicky's bath and bedtime routine, Monica drifted out onto the porch again. She both hoped and feared to find Zach there, and spotted him immediately.

With one foot propped on the railing's sturdy timber and an elbow propped on the bent knee, he was smoking a cigar. And looking way too attractive for her peace of mind, Monica thought while her pulse did this little skippy thing she wished it wouldn't do.

He turned his head. "Hi."

"Hi, yourself." Returning his smile, ignoring her pulse, she went over to him and hitched herself into a sitting position upon the foot-thick beam. "I didn't know you smoked," she observed, appreciatively sniffing the rich aroma even though she didn't approve of smoking as a rule.

"I don't." Zach took the cigar from his mouth and blew out a perfect smoke ring. He acknowledged Monica's silent applause with an inclination of his head. "Except when there's something to celebrate."

"And there is, isn't there," Monica said dreamily, tilting her head so that her temple rested against the pillar that supported her shoulder. "I can't begin to tell you, how much—"

"Then do me a favor and don't," Zach interrupted. "You've thanked me enough. It's embarrassing."

"Embarrassing?" Monica's head snapped away from the pillar and she stared at him with exasperated incredulity. "For *you* it's embarrassing? What about me?"

"What about you?"

Monica rolled her eyes. "I'm not allowed to pay. I'm not allowed to work. I feel like a freeloader."

"You want to work?" Zach puffed and expelled another ring, wondering if he was crazy offering her a job. She'd be around him, closely around him, even more than she was already. Would he be able to handle that okay?

Worse, would he be able to handle her leaving—as she most certainly would—once he'd gotten used to having her around?

"I need a secretary," he said gruffly, because he felt pretty sure he was making a terrible mistake. "My current one is retiring. Now, in off-season, the job'd take about two days a week of your time."

"We-ell..." Monica bit her lip in an agony of indecision. The idea of being with Zach, working with him, in close proximity, was both tempting and scary. What if she got used to it, to him, to this place, this life? Would she be able to just walk away, as she knew very well she'd sooner or later have to?

"Think about it." No longer feeling celebratory after Monica's hesitant response, Zach tossed the cigar into a half-dried puddle on the other side of the porch. "Don't say anything right now. Because there's something Becky mentioned that I think you need to know."

He took his foot off the railing and turned to lean back against it, folding his arms. Though she sat some two feet away from him, he was acutely aware of her, her by-now-familiar scent conjuring an image of summer meadows and moonlight swims...

Moonlight swims? Get a grip, old man. Zach shifted his stance and took a deep breath. He wished now he'd kept hold of the damned cigar. He wished he could convince her she'd fit in well here at Windemeer. He wished he could convince her to trust him with the full story of her flight from the little girl's father, because some instinct told him she was holding something back.

And he wished he could convince her that he'd make a helluva good stepdad for her precious little girl.

"You're safe here," he said, which wasn't what he'd meant to say. "I just want you to know that. And you're welcome to stay for as long as you like, work or no work. Anybody wants to find you, and you don't want to be found…" With a shrug, he let the sentence hang and slanted her a glance. Not surprisingly, he saw Monica's eyes widen with alarm.

She asked, "What aren't you telling me?"

Zach, annoyed with himself for the clumsy way he was going about all this, blew out a hard breath. "A man came to Becky's office, asking if she knew where you were."

Even in the gathering gloom of dusk, he could see the color drain from Monica's face. He saw her swallow, but her voice came out as a ragged croak anyway when she asked, "A…man?"

"Tallish, balding, flashy dresser," Zach recited like a laundry list, using Becky's terms almost verbatim.

Monica felt as if she'd been whacked across the midsection with one of the porch timbers. She lowered her chin to her chest and hugged her middle, fighting down nausea. And fear. Such fear.

"Richard," she whispered tonelessly. "He's found us." She raised her head, panic now in every line of her face. "Oh, dear God. He's found us!"

"No, he hasn't." Zach didn't even realize he'd moved until he felt his fingers close around her upper arms. Sensing approaching hysteria, he gave her a little shake. "He has not found you, Monica. Look at me."

He waited until Monica complied before going on. "Becky told him she had no idea where you were. And she was telling the truth, because she didn't know." He shook her again, gently, for emphasis. "Right? You understand? She did not know."

"Yes…" Monica's eyes clung to his. Anxiety had widened them, and the reflection from the setting sun turned them to gold. "She *didn't* know…"

"That's right."

Monica blinked. "But she knows now, doesn't she?"

"So what?" Letting go of her arms, Zach caught her face between his two hands when she would have turned it away. "Even if he does show up again at her office, which why the heck he should I've no idea, Rebecca would never tell. Not if she's convinced there's a good reason for her not to."

Monica's eyes searched his. She thought she detected something there, a doubt? A question?

"And are you wondering," she whispered slowly, "if there is good reason?"

"No…"

"Yes!" Feeling cornered, knowing she owed him the truth but scared, so scared, Monica responded with bluster. She wrenched her face out of Zach's hands and jumped off the railing. She stalked a few steps and spun.

"All this talk of simple kindness and compassion," she accused. "All this goodwill, this offer of a job… It all depends, doesn't it? On whether I'm worthy. On whether I am who I say. On whether things are as they seem!"

She stopped him when Zach would have interrupted. "I'll bet you're thinking, She must've done *something* if her ex-husband's chasing her like this! Well, all right…"

She stared at him with burning eyes. Such tortured eyes, that Zach would gladly have made her stop.

But he realized it was too late for that, when, in a tired voice, she admitted, "I did do something! I rescued my child. I rescued her from certain hell, from being abandoned to a fate worse than death!"

When Zach only stood there, struggling to comprehend, she walked away, stared into the night. "Sounds melodramatic, doesn't it?'' She gave a bitter little laugh. "It wasn't. It was almost frighteningly easy.''

"What was?'' Zach asked, because he failed to grasp just what, exactly, she had done.

"Kidnapping my child.''

"What!''

She made herself face him. "You're harboring a criminal, Zach. I'm sorry. We'll be leaving—''

"Stop it,'' Zach interrupted with one hand raised. The fingers of the other one speared into his hair as he struggled to assimilate what he'd just heard. He looked at Monica.

Her head was bent now; one hand was over her eyes. One arm was hugging her middle. She looked...depleted.

With a sigh, he dropped his hands. "I think,'' he said, "that you owe it to me to start from the top.''

"All right.'' Monica tiredly dropped her hand and hugged herself with both arms. "Ask me anything.''

"Why?'' The question was uppermost in Zach's mind.

Monica swallowed; the horror of Richard's plans still gave her nightmares. "He was going to have her committed.'' She bit her lip. "To an institution.''

Shock kept Zach momentarily immobile. An *institution?* "But...why?''

"For money.''

"Money?'' Zach repeated incredulously. "What money?'' Had he missed something here? "I thought you said you had no money.''

"I don't. Nicole does.''

"Nicole?''

"Yes.'' Monica closed her eyes. If only her head would stop throbbing maybe she'd be able to explain things more coherently. "It's a trust fund set up by Richard's father. This was before Richard ran the real estate company into the ground.''

"How much?''

"The principal is a quarter million.''

Zach gave a soundless whistle. "That ain't hay."

Monica didn't react. She massaged her temples. "The money comes to her at twenty-one. In the meantime, neither of us can touch it. Except..."

"Except?" Zach prompted when Monica faltered, although a terrible premonition of what that exception would be was beginning to dawn.

"Richard. As the fund's executor, he is also its sole beneficiary should Nicky...die or somehow be judged..."

"Mentally incompetent," Zach finished in a shocked, ragged whisper when Monica's breath hitched and she let the sentence hang.

Her, "Yes," was almost inaudible.

"My God." Zach was stunned. He'd thought he'd seen it all, heard it all. But this... How low could a man sink? A father... To try to do such dirt to a helpless little girl. His own flesh and blood... It was beyond comprehension.

And Monica...

He looked over to where she stood with her hand once again over her eyes and her head bowed. Brave, intrepid Monica... A criminal? Not in his mind.

He went over to her. He stood behind her, would have liked to touch her, pull her against him and tell her she wasn't alone. But something about the stillness with which she held herself made him stuff his hands into his own pockets instead.

"How come," he asked after clearing his throat a few times, "that she was with him in the first place? And how'd you find out about...his plans?"

Monica dropped her hand. Her eyes, meeting Zach's, were huge, and filled with despair. She looked wan and vulnerable. And, to Zach, utterly beautiful.

Behind her, beyond the porch, it was full dark now. A narrow crescent moon hung low on the horizon. The only illumination came from the light spilling out of the living room window. Zach figured Ada must have gone in and turned on a lamp.

Monica shivered and wrapped her arms around herself.

He touched her then, just his hand on her arm. "You're cold. Let's go inside."

"No." Monica shook her head. "Please. I'm all right."

Zach doubted that, but didn't push. Instead he put his arm around her shoulders and led her to a bench against the wall that was sheltered from the breeze coming off the water.

He urged her down on it and sat beside her. "Feel like telling me the rest? You don't have to," he added quickly, "unless you want to."

"I do." Monica figured she owed it to him to make a clean breast of things now. Once he knew, well...

She took a breath. "Nicky was on a court-appointed visitation with Richard. I'm the primary custodian, but he...gets to see her several times a year."

Sensing Zach's question, she elaborated, "You see, I never told anyone about his...excesses, never pressed...charges."

She flattened her lips, regretting as she had so many, many times the naiveté that had made her believe that divorce would be enough.

"I was stupid, and ashamed." Bitterly, she added, "And my child is paying the price."

She took Zach's silence for well-deserved condemnation, though in reality Zach was remembering that in his case, too, a child had paid the price. And that, as a consequence, he'd be the last person to judge what this woman had done.

"So anyway," Monica forced herself to continue, "Richard had moved to Spokane after the divorce, and pretty much left us alone. I was glad. With the business itself gone, I worked some out of our home. This thing with Rebecca, stuff like that. Anything that would allow me stay home with Nicole.

"Everything was going along pretty good. Nicky was...well, I thought she was improving. And then, out of the blue, Richard wanted her in Spokane. I tried to stall, but…''

Monica spread her hands in a motion of helplessness and continued to look down at them. "He had the law on his side and he simply came and took her. Three weeks, he said. I was…frantic.''

She closed her hands into fists, remembering. "And I completely went off the deep end when, around the middle of the second week, I get this fax, several pages. They turned out to be copies of…the commitment papers that Richard had had drawn up. The cover letter, unsigned, simply said that I might find the attached of interest. And also gave me the name and address of a baby-sitter where Nicole, apparently, was staying. I was on the next plane over there.''

"Wow.'' Zach expelled a not-quite-steady breath. He turned his head to look at her. She had tipped back her head so that it rested against the wall. Her eyes were once again closed. Even here in the shadows, he could see that she was utterly drained.

"You don't have to say anything more,'' he told her quietly.

Monica sighed. "There isn't much more to tell, anyway. I wasn't really rational. I called Mom, and she took care of some things in Seattle and was there for us when we got back.

"In Spokane, there was this woman. The baby-sitter…'' Monica faltered. She hated to remember that she'd done violence to a woman who didn't deserve it, whose only fault had been to do her duty and thus to get in the way of an outraged mother. "I, um… I…locked her in the bathroom.''

"Incredible.'' Zach shook his head in amazement. Was every mother as fiercely protective of her child? Had his own mother been, when she was still alive? He'd been so young when his parents were killed, only six years old. Becky, a whole six years older, had been his surrogate mom, even as they bounced from foster home to foster home.

And, yes, she would have fought for him just as hard as Monica was fighting for Nicole.

Interpreting Zach's silence for censure, Monica's head snapped away from the wall. She looked fiercely into his eyes. "I would do it again," she said. "Everything."

And choked on a shocked little gasp when Zach grabbed her by the shoulders, kissed her hard on the mouth, and released her with a heartfelt, "Good for you!"

"What?" She stared at him in consternation. "You can't mean that!"

"Oh, but I do."

"I committed a felony."

"I know."

"But..." She searched his eyes; was shocked when she thought she saw humor. "Don't you care?"

"Not really."

"Well, you darn well should." Too upset by what she saw as his failure to appreciate the grievous wrong she'd done him by accepting his hospitality, Monica surged off the bench.

"We have to leave." She said the words at the same time she was making the decision, knowing it was the right—the only—decision to make. "We have to be gone from here before he tracks us to Windemeer."

"Don't be ridiculous." Zach, too, was on his feet. All traces of humor had vanished. "You can't just keep on running. Have you thought what it would do to Nicole?"

"Of course I have. This is all about Nicole. But what other choice is there?"

"You could stay here."

"And incriminate you more than I have already? Oh, Zach..."

Zach ignored her reproachful shake of the head. He caught her hands in his and said, "Monica. Look at me."

And when she did, he said, ''Do you like it here? Does Nicole?''

Monica frowned. What was he trying to do, make her cry? ''Well, of course we like it here. It's been wonderful here...''

''Then stay,'' Zach said. ''And marry me.''

Chapter Six

Monica stared at him. "You can't be serious."

"Oh, I'm serious, all right." Zach looked hard into Monica's eyes. "I want you to know that I've only ever asked one other woman to marry me. And that she'd be the first to tell you she was a fool for accepting. I'm no prize…"

"What a thing to say!" the romantic in Monica felt compelled to protest. She might not have had moonshine and roses in her own marriage, but that didn't mean she wasn't a firm believer that other people should. And did. She'd hardly have gone into the dating business if she didn't believe that true love was out there, even if not for her.

"I'm sure she was madly in love with you. And you with her."

"Well…" Zach chuckled humorlessly. "Let's just say we thought we were and let it go at that."

He cleared his throat, thinking he was making a pretty fine mess out of convincing her to stay. He decided he'd better stop pussyfooting around and get to the point. "The bottom line is, I don't want you to go."

When Monica didn't react in any way, he compressed his lips against a surge of bitterness. *Stupid old fool, you've embarrassed her.* He let go of her hands, and didn't comment when she immediately moved away.

Monica needed to move, to put some distance between herself and this man who, though he didn't seem to know it, had the power to stir her in ways no man had been able to since—

No, she amended, striding to the other side of the porch where a latticed wall broke the force of the wind gusts that had grown increasingly stronger. Not even in the days when Richard was courting her had she felt the way Zach could make her feel with very little effort.

Zach would be a wonderful friend. Good grief, even on their short acquaintance he'd shown her more caring and consideration than Richard had in all of the seven years they were together.

He would be a marvelous, a stupendous father, too. Just look at the way Nicky was already responding to him.

And he'd be a great lover, too, she thought, not daring to as much as glance in his direction lest he read what she was thinking. He'd be tender, but passionate, as well. Why else would she be feeling his eyes on her even now, like a searing caress all the way across the porch?

There was so much about Zach, in Zach, that called to her. That touched something. Stirred *something.* Something she'd come to believe she lacked. Something restless. And wild. Passion?

She closed her eyes and admitted to herself that, yes, that was it. Zach could make her feel passion and, God help her, if she weren't careful he could all too easily make her feel…*love.*

With every passing second, as he watched Monica's inner struggle and the silence between them lengthened, Zach cursed himself for having spoken.

All the more so when, finally, she looked at him almost pleadingly and whispered, "I can't, Zach. I...just can't."

Monica fervently hoped Zach would accept that and let it go.

But he didn't. He swallowed his pride. "It wouldn't have to be a real marriage," he said. "I'm not asking you to love me. Hell, I'm fourteen years older and—"

"Your age has nothing to do with it!" Monica vehemently interrupted, with tears clogging her throat. "And I'm not saying no because you wouldn't be easy to love. Don't you see?"

She went to him. Gripped his arms and looked up at him. "It's precisely because it would be so very easy to fall in...love with you that I can't—

"Oh, Zach, wait!" she exclaimed, resisting when he shrugged off her hands and, cupping her shoulders, tried to tug her body closer to his. "Let me finish. Please."

Zach said nothing, didn't move. Just held her and looked at her, searching her eyes, which were like shiny amber, overbright with unshed tears, and full of desperate entreaty.

"All I am," she said urgently, willing him to understand, "all the feelings I am capable of, have to go to Nicky right now. Only to Nicky. Until she's safe, and until she's well again, I can't even begin to think of loving anyone else. Not even you, whose kindness I would give anything to be able to repay."

"Repay?" Zach stared at her, aghast. "I don't want repayment. I want to help, to keep you safe, and to give that little girl of yours a chance. I agree that she's the one who's most important here. And you know why?"

Monica mutely shook her head.

"Because she's an innocent." Zach's tone grew more intense. His grip on Monica's shoulders grew almost painful. "She's a true innocent who didn't ask for the hand that was dealt her but is stuck with playing it, just the same. Because of us! Because of our mistakes, our choices, our selfishness and—

"Damn!" He abruptly let go of her and swung away. Putting a hand over his eyes, he struggled to beat back the tide of guilt and self-recrimination that had nothing to do with the present and everything to do with the past.

"Zach…" Shaken, and hesitant to intrude on his visibly raw emotions, Monica put a hand on his arm. "You're not just talking about Nicky here, are you?"

"No."

She didn't think he would say anything else, he was silent for so long. Feeling helpless, Monica watched his jaw clench and unclench in an outward indication of some powerful inner struggle.

"I'm talking about Maddy," he finally said in a tone of such desolation it squeezed the blood right out of Monica's heart. "My own…little girl."

He walked to the railing and stared up at a sky whose wind-whipped turbulence aptly mirrored his emotions. "I killed her."

Dear God. Monica pressed both hands to her mouth to stifle her gasp. Had she heard him right?

"If you'll let me tell you about it, maybe you'll see why it's so important to me for Nicole to be safe."

"Go on," Monica said, though hesitantly.

Zach took a breath. "Sarah, my wife, was out."

Zach kept his voice carefully flat. He knew that if he didn't, he'd never get this told, and it was important that he did. It was important for Monica to hear every word, to know who he had been and who he was now. And to know of the demons that haunted him.

"Sarah partied a lot. Hell, we both did. This particular night, though, I volunteered to stay home and baby-sit. The nanny had an emergency or some such. Whatever. I liked being a dad. I liked to read to Maddy, play games with her, fool around.

"On my own terms, of course," he added in a tone of

bitter self-mockery. "After all, I was a busy man, an idol, a *basketball star.*"

He instilled the term with utter loathing. And when he turned, Monica was shocked by his ravaged expression. He buried his hands in his pockets. His voice constricted.

"Maddy had the flu," he said. "A temperature. Just like Nicole the other day. I put her to bed and read her some *Winnie-The-Pooh.* Later, I sat in the den and watched some TV, keeping myself amused in what had become my usual fashion. Some Scotch, maybe a few pills... Whatever it took to make me forget how much I despised the person I had become. Pretty soon I passed out. Only way I *could* get to sleep in those days."

Zach stopped. He squinted at Monica's pale face. "Are you shocked yet? Disgusted?"

"No," she said, not quite truthfully. She was shocked, yes, but only because she was unable to reconcile the reality of the man she had come to know and respect with the craven, dissolute caricature of a man he was conjuring up with his words.

A caricature that was distressingly, frighteningly reminiscent of Richard Sinclair.

"Well, let me tell you the rest and you will be," Zach said with profound self-disgust. He turned back to the night; he really didn't want to see Monica's expression when he told her the rest.

"It seems she woke up during the night, Maddy did, burning up with fever. Crying. But, of course, nobody heard her. My lovely wife never did make it home that night, and I, good ol' daddy, was out of my mind so that I didn't wake up when...my little girl...needed me. And when I did wake up, the next morning, because the nanny was standing there, screaming, it was...too late. Maddy was...gone."

Zach's throat closed. He drew a tortured breath. "I wanted to die. And later, when strings were pulled by Sarah's influential family so that no charges were ever filed, I did try every which way to kill myself with more booze and more pills. It was Becky who stopped me, again and again. She wouldn't let me take the coward's way out.

"And I hated her for it. Until one day it dawned on me. This was my punishment. Staying alive when my little girl was dead was my purgatory."

He turned and gazed down at Monica who could barely breathe past the awful constriction in her throat. "It's been twenty years, Monica. Twenty years of remorse, of trying to make up for my negligence. I've changed. And I truly believe that by helping you and Nicole I've been given another chance…to make amends. So please…"

He moved a step closer but didn't touch her. "All I ask is that you give me an opportunity to do things right this time. You name the terms."

"Is that offer still open?" Monica asked shakily after a while, after they had looked into each other's eyes and hearts for a long, long time during which they acknowledged that their relationship had moved to a different level.

A level of intimacy that had nothing to do with the physical, but, instead, accepted that they both had suffered, that they had both made mistakes—grievous ones. Irreversible ones. But that they were united now in a common goal—Nicole's safety and well-being.

"Which offer?" Zach asked, taking Monica's hands and looking down at them. "I recall making you two—full-time wife or part-time secretary."

"And I appreciate both of those offers more than I can say. The trouble is…" Monica bit her lip with a wobbly little smile. "I've been a wife, and I wasn't very good at it. But I've never been a secretary…."

"All right then." Not for the world was Zach going to let on how much he had hoped she would choose to accept the other offer. She was staying. And that was something. A start.

Labor Day weekend had long since come and gone. The season, with its hunting trips, fishing trips, excursions by plane to the Barren Islands or wherever else some rich man's fancy took them and the services of Windemeer Charters, was irrevocably over.

The weather wasted no time letting them know that fall had arrived and that winter was not far behind. The wind whistled around the assortment of buildings that Windemeer consisted of, and the rain came down sideways. Apparently without ever again wanting to stop.

The confidences Monica and Zach had exchanged that night on the porch were never alluded to again. But the understandings they had reached influenced their every thought and action.

"Is this what we're faced with from now until spring?" Monica asked one morning over breakfast. Outside, the wind was rattling the windows and rain pelted the glass like so many handfuls of tossed pebbles. She and Nicole had been cooped up in the house for days and they were both getting restless.

"Heck, no." Zach exchanged a glance with Ada that made Monica's antennae stand up. She'd learned by now that these two sometimes gruff and taciturn people had a mischievous streak as wide as a mile.

"Couldn't stand it, if it did," Ada said. "Nothin' like a good blizzard for a change o' pace."

"A blizzard. Gee, thanks." Monica turned to Nicky who was quietly rearranging alphabet cereal in the bottom of her bowl. "Though at least we could go out and build a snowman then, couldn't we?"

Nicole's eyes kindled with interest and she gave an emphatic nod. But Monica barely acknowledged it. Her own eyes were riveted on the cereal letters Nicky had lined up—M-O-M.

"Nicky," she gasped, staring at her child with an expression of incredulous delight. "You made a *word*. Zach, Ada, come and see…"

Jubilant, she framed her daughter's face and kissed her

smack on her sticky little mouth. "You're wonderful! Oh, sweetheart, I'm so proud of you!"

"And so am I." Zach ruffled the girl's hair and announced, "This calls for a celebration! Who wants to come with me into town?"

"Town." Monica drew the word out in a tone of surprise. This would be their first time away from Windemeer since they arrived. "You mean, go into Kodiak with you?"

"Only town around here worth going to on a day like this."

"Oh. Well." Monica looked questioningly at her daughter. She'd be ashamed to admit it, but the truth was she wanted desperately to go, Nicole or no. Though she would never complain, and though she enjoyed being with Nicky, teaching her, playing with her, reading to her, and though she rejoiced in every bit of progress, she was more than ready for a break.

It was tough being a single parent, even at the best of times. At the worst of times, which her particular situation came pretty darned close to being, it was terrifying and utterly exhausting.

Add to that the undeniable currents of awareness and tension vibrating between Zach and herself, and there were times when Monica felt as though her turbulent and conflicting emotions were like a bubbling cauldron of witch's brew ready to explode at the slightest provocation. Explode and shatter her into a billion pieces, all of which would puddle in a heap of fragments at Zach Robinson's feet.

The fact that at those times she would catch herself wondering if Zach would scatter her remains with one swift kick of his size fifteens, or carefully gather them up and try to put her back together was—to her—proof positive that she was skating precariously close to the edge.

And so... Monica sighed. Was she ready for a break? Lord, yes. But more than that, she was dying for a chance to not just be a mom for a few hours, but also a woman.

A woman enjoying the company of a man. Herself enjoying the company of one particular man—Zach Robinson.

Yet there could be no question, of course, of leaving Nicky behind. True, the child was becoming every day more outgoing in her silent, stoic way. And she had begun to trust Ada and Mitch—thanks mostly to Zelda's litter of puppies—as well as having become truly attached to Zach who had a wonderful way with her. But always knowing that her mother was nearby.

"What d'you think, sweetheart? Town? Cars and trucks, people, stores for shopping? Maybe go see Grandma?" she added on a flash of inspiration while darting a quick glance at Zach for confirmation.

Zach nodded. He was touched by Monica's almost palpable eagerness. And though it was for safety reasons she and the child had stayed close to home, he called himself all kinds of an idiot for not having realized before that she might relish a change. He shared her pleased relief, therefore, when Nicky vigorously nodded and shot off the chair, holding out her hand as if to say, "Let's go."

"Hey, whoa, there, young lady." Monica pointedly picked up her own place setting and started toward the sink with it. "Haven't you forgotten something?"

For a moment it looked as though Nicky might balk. Zach caught himself holding his breath. He was tempted to interfere, to say, "Let it go," and could see Ada fighting the same inclination.

He was glad they both had kept quiet when, with a very put-upon and audible sigh, Nicole picked up her cereal bowl and spoon and, her rabbit firmly clamped beneath one arm, marched with it to the sink.

"Thank you, sweetheart," Monica said serenely, patting the child's head, but exchanging a glance with Zach that clearly showed relief.

This wasn't the first such stand-off. With her sense of security growing and the walls behind which she had hidden her "self" slowly but surely beginning to crumble, Nicole's innate sense of autonomy was growing stronger, as well. She was no longer quite the docile, almost robot-like creature she'd been.

"Old Ada sure appreciates your help, Nicky," Ada praised. "Maybe tomorrow you could help me bake cookies again. You think?"

Nicky spared her a quick nod and hurried after her mother, who was saying, "Just as soon as we've washed our hands and brushed our teeth, Zach, we'll be ready to go."

"Better bundle yourself and that child up good," Ada squawked fussily, trotting after them. "Liable to have a relapse, you're not careful...." This even though it had been more than a month since their illness.

Duly slickered and booted, Zach had just gotten them settled in the Suburban—a newer version of the one he'd driven in Anchorage which, he had explained to Monica, he kept at the airfield there for city use—when Nicky shot out of her seat and ran back to Ada who was hovering at the stoop and still fussing.

"Nicky!" Monica's startled protest coincided with Zach's. She moved to follow the child, but Zach stayed her. Together they watched in wonder as Nicky whipped the rabbit out from beneath her slicker and put it in Ada's hands. Then she urged the old woman's arm upward until Ada was cradling the stuffed toy just right, nodded with obvious satisfaction and dashed back into the truck.

Amazed, Monica couldn't say a word; she just silently moved her legs aside to let Nicky squeeze in between Zach and herself. When she trusted her voice to be steady, she said, "That was very nice of you, Nicky, to give Ada your bunny for company."

She hugged the child to her, but her eyes sought Zach's in grateful communication.

He made no audible reply, but his facial expression left no doubt as to where *he* thought the credit belonged.

Driving along at a sedate speed, Zach found he very much enjoyed the idea that people in town who didn't know who he was—and, admittedly, there weren't too many—might think he was just another family man out with his wife and kid. And if those folks who did know him assumed that Monica was his *girlfriend*—why that was fine with him, too.

Her scent was all around him. Even with Nicky between them, he was keenly aware of her with every atom of his being. For the umpteenth time since they'd left home, he glanced at her over Nicole's coppery head.

And caught her this time gazing at him with an expression in her eyes that made him want to slam on the brakes, haul her into his arms and kiss the breath out of her.

His blood surged hotly in response to this urge, making him squirm. It didn't help that Monica blushed to the roots of her hair and hastily looked straight ahead. He'd seen what he'd seen—desire. And it gave him hope.

To divert his thoughts into a safer and, given the circumstances, more appropriate direction, he pointed out some of the sights and historical points of interest. He was proud of his adopted hometown. The community's history was rich and varied, its heritage evident even now, some two hundred years after the days when the Russian Empire in the North Pacific had been administered from Kodiak.

"You two missed the State Fair, of course," he informed "his" two ladies. "But there's a pretty decent Oktoberfest just around the corner."

"Oktoberfest doesn't sound very Russian." Monica, her pulse still racing from the electrifying mesh of her gaze with Zach's, carefully avoided further eye contact. She craned her neck for a better view of a quaint church with blue onion-bulb towers. "That church…"

"Is called Holy Resurrection," Zach supplied. "It's Russian Orthodox. And over there—" he pointed "—is the Baranov Mansion, so called after Alexander Baranov who got things started around here in the mid-seventeen hundreds. The townsfolk got together and restored it a coupl'a decades ago.''

"Wow." Gradually relaxing even though Zach's apparent calm made her wonder if she'd imagined the flash of potent heat in the gaze that had held her own, Monica felt like a tourist. And she was thrilled to see that Nicole, too, was looking around with wide-eyed interest. There was no sign now of the withdrawn little child who used to dully stare out at the world, if taking note of it, at all.

If only she would speak, Monica thought wistfully. There were times when it seemed as though she was just about to. Times when her lips moved while she looked at a picture book, as if her mouth were shaping words. But maybe that was just wishful thinking.

When she's ready to talk, she'll talk. When it's important enough to her, she'll talk. That's what Doc Koontz said, and that's what Monica clung to.

"So what's the agenda?" she asked as they cruised down Center Avenue, looking for a place to park. The rain had stopped, though the wind hadn't lessened, and Zach had suggested it might be nice to stretch their legs, look around.

"First off," Zach said, catching Nicky's eye while, at the same time, heading for the parking slot he'd just spotted a little ways up the block, "I was hoping that a certain little girl would maybe like an ice cream cone...

"What do you think, Mom?" he queried, expertly positioning his big rig in a slot so compact, Monica wouldn't have attempted to park even the little Honda she used to own in it. "Do we have a little girl like that with us here?

"Oh," he exclaimed, deadpan when Nicole tugged on his sleeve. "Of course we do. Nicky! You've been so quiet, I forgot you were here! Well, come, then. What're we waiting for?"

He slid out of the truck, strode around to the other side and got there just in time to scoop Nicky up and spin her around once while Monica stood on the sidewalk with what she knew had to be a dopey grin on her face. She couldn't help it—every time she saw Zach with her daughter, happiness of a kind she'd never thought possible filled her to bursting.

He was so good. And he had gone through so much. It gave her no end of pleasure and satisfaction to be able to play a part in helping him heal. The knowledge that he wanted her to play an even greater part in his life—the role of *wife*—pleasured her, too.

Almost as much as it pained her to acknowledge that with Nicky so needy, and with Richard on their trail, it was a role she would never be able to do more than dream about.

They ate ice cream cones and telephoned the Romanovs, but didn't get an answer. "Next time," Zach said, consolingly, "we'll call ahead and set something up."

They shopped till they dropped—mostly for clothes for Nicole who was growing like a weed and needed winter things and such. Zach would have paid for it all, but Monica wouldn't allow it.

"No way," she said flatly. "Bad enough you insist on paying me for the office work I do, when *I* should be paying you room and board."

They also bought some videos to watch at home and filled the grocery order Ada had sent along. They went to the drugstore where Monica needed some things.

Back out on the street, she declared, "I don't know about you two but I, for one, am starving. Lunch is on me," she told Zach. "No arguments!

"So." She turned to Nicole. "What do we feel like?" She knew what the answer would be, of course, even without words, since she had strategically chosen to pose the question while standing in front of a pizza parlor.

Pizza was something Nicky adored and Ada refused to make. "I'm Inuit," she had huffily proclaimed when Monica had asked for it on Nicky's behalf. "Not Italian. I don't do pizza."

Unfortunately, the other thing she didn't do was share her kitchen. Monica had thus far not been allowed to prepare a meal.

So now it was a foregone conclusion that Nicky would choose pizza for lunch. Looking very pleased with herself, she grabbed each adult by the hand and dragged them inside.

After lunch Zach made them stop at the pet shop where Nicky marveled at the animals and got to hold a gerbil. She then proceeded to appall her mother—who had an abiding horror of any and all rodents—by indicating her desire to keep it.

"Oh, no, darling, you can't." Monica tossed a reproving glance at Zach who, to her way of thinking, had instigated this crisis by dragging them into this place. "Remember we've got kitties at home? Kitties don't like gerbils. Do they, Zach?" she added, her narrowed eyes daring him not to concur.

Zach noted the look, thought she looked cute, and said the right thing. "Ah...no." He hunkered down in front of Nicole, brought his mouth to her ear and whispered something that made Nicole's eyes widen with delight. She promptly put down the gerbil, took hold of Zach's hand and dragged him toward a display of dog paraphernalia.

Monica, astounded, was left to follow or not. Her astonishment grew when her daughter selected a glaringly pink collar with matching leash.

"Now what in the world..." Monica couldn't believe Zach was actually paying for Nicole's selections. "Neither Zelda nor Zeus would be caught dead in those things!"

"Zeus or Zelda?" Zach chuckled. He winked at Nicky. "Mom's funny, isn't she?"

Beaming, hugging the bag with her purchases to her chest, Nicole nodded. Giggled.

Giggled?

Bewildered, delighted, and maddeningly close to a silly

bout of tears, Monica struggled to play along with whatever game this confounding, bewildering, but, oh, so compelling man and this very small girl were playing.

"All right, you two," she demanded with mock severity. "Who's the lead and the collar for?"

The two conspirators looked at each other and grinned. "Should I tell her?" Zach asked. And after Nicky's vigorous nod, added, "Why, they're for Nicky's new puppy, of course."

Chapter Seven

"So what are you gonna name him, toots?" Zach asked Nicole who, along with Monica and himself was hunkered down in the corner of the barn where Mitch Gordon had set up Zelda's nursery. The pups weren't quite weaned yet and it would be another week or two before the rest of the litter would be put up for sale, but Nicole had been given the runt of the litter, an adorable ball of fur no bigger than Zach's hand.

It took both of Nicole's hands, however, and all of her concentration to hang on to the squirming little bundle in the way Zach had demonstrated.

Now, startled by Zach's question, the big brown eyes that had until then adoringly gazed at her new charge swung inquiringly toward her mother.

"Better put on your thinking cap," Monica gasped, laughing and trying to dodge one adventurous tyke's busy tongue. The little guy had climbed up her chest and was enthusiastically bestowing doggie kisses.

Zach envied the pup. These days he thought a lot about

kisses. Kisses, and more. Much more. And always with this woman. Only with this woman.

He sighed. For in spite of that look he'd intercepted in the car on their way to town, that look of wistful longing and unmistakable desire, he was enough of a realist to know that *thinking* about making love with Monica was probably as much as he'd ever get to do. He was trying to come to terms with that. And at times could almost convince himself that he had. For whole minutes at a time...

Or maybe he was going about it all wrong. Maybe coming to terms was not what he should be doing. Maybe it was time to change tactics, time to act on the emotions she'd inadvertently let him catch a glimpse of. Time to simply catch her, hold her, kiss her, and *show* her how it could be between the two of them. Maybe then she would say yes to his proposal, and stay here with him. And be his wife.

Another sigh, this one of chagrined resignation because he knew it wasn't in him to make a pass, or in any way coerce Monica to his way of thinking. He'd go on just as he had been, do just what he had been doing. And that was to wait. And hope. And do his damnedest to keep her and little Nicky safe.

In the meantime, however, he'd best get his mind back to the matter at hand, and that was to get that little girl to talk because, like Monica, he had become totally convinced that she could. That the payoff just had to be big enough. It had occurred to him that a puppy of her own just might fit the bill and, judging by the look on Nicky's face, he'd hit the nail right on the head.

"Mitch's rule," he told her now. "You don't get to take the puppy back to the house with you unless you give him a name so you can call him," he said. "Otherwise how's he gonna know you want him to come? Say, if he got lost. It's a big place out here and it'll be your job to look out for him. Just like Mommy looks out for you."

Nicole, hugging the puppy within an inch of its life, was

visibly digesting all of this. Her brow furrowed. And then cleared. With an air of triumph, she pointed at Zelda.

"Oh, no." Zach didn't even pretend not to understand. "Once the puppy's old enough to be yours all the time, Zelda won't look out for him anymore. That's just the way it is."

Watching the little girl's eyes cloud and the forehead once again crease in a pucker, Zach decided they had pushed the issue enough for now.

"C'mon," he said, putting his own little charges back with Mama Zelda and pushing to his feet. "The puppies are tired." He reached out a hand to help Monica up. As always, even a casual touch such as this generated enough electricity to make the hairs on his arm stand up.

Avoiding each other's eyes, they were both dusting themselves off and picking at dog hairs when a little voice, rusty from disuse and not very clearly said, "Char-lie."

Monica froze. Everything else forgotten, her eyes, widening with a kind of hopeful disbelief, connected with Zach's for one breathless moment. And then they both swung around to stare speechlessly at Nicole.

She was still on her knees in the straw nest that was Zelda's nursery. Effort and stubborn determination puckered the high forehead behind a disheveled fringe of coppery bangs. But the look in the eyes that gazed up at the adults was one of pure triumph as she repeated, more clearly, the puppy's new name. "Char-lie...."

When the weather cleared a few days later and the forecast promised conditions would hold, Zach got in one of his Cessnas and flew to Anchorage. With him he carried the lengthy list Monica had drawn up. Aside from a whole plethora of educational items from the Learning Store, it included her request for a specific sewing pattern and fabric for matching Halloween costumes for herself and Nicky. And, he wryly reminded himself, for him.

Though he had barked an adamant, "No way," when

Monica had first told him they wanted him to dress up, too, he had, as usual, caved in when confronted by two crestfallen female faces.

Questioning Nicky's readiness to venture into, let alone participate, in the potentially scary revelry of ghosts and goblins hadn't done him any good, either.

"Depending on how she copes," Monica had told him, "we can either just watch the trick-or-treaters at Mom's house or go out ourselves. But either way, we'll all want to be in costume."

"What I wouldn't give to be able to see the three of you." Becky, who had accompanied Zach on this—to him, daunting—shopping excursion, let the front door of her business, Searching Singles, fall shut behind her with an amused shake of her head. "Dalmatians! What a hoot..."

"I know." Zach responded to her chuckle with a sheepish grin. "The two of *them* are gonna look cute as all get out and I'm gonna look ridiculous." He shrugged. "I guess the fact that I'm not going to worry about it tells you something about my state of mind."

"That it does," Becky teased with an arched glance across her shoulder. "I'm not sure what, though."

"Ha, ha," Zach countered without rancor.

In the course of their morning together, his sister had repeatedly tried to extract from him as much information about him and his houseguests as she could. He had answered selectively, sometimes evasively. For even though he knew that concern, not idle curiosity, prompted her probing questions, he had felt it imperative to guard Monica's privacy.

Becky being Becky, she had accepted his reticence with grudging grace. And a little while later, tried a different tack only to find it didn't get her anywhere, either.

Now, trailing her past the cozy sitting area at the front of the twenty-by-twenty-eight-foot area occupied by Searching Singles, Zach fondly eyed her compact form and decided that when it came to sisters, he could have done worse.

As he walked past the two computer-topped desks that were the workstations of Rebecca's two employees, he nodded and smiled at Dora Miles, a bespectacled, spinsterish woman in her late thirties. Dora didn't match Zach's image of a dating service representative but according to Becky, she was a business dynamo.

At the moment she was on the phone and returned Zach's silent greeting with even more than her usual self-conscious nervousness.

Or maybe he was just imagining that, Zach thought, more embarrassed than flattered, because he knew from Rebecca that Dora supposedly had a crush on him. He wished Becky hadn't told him because, true or not, even in the days of his so-called stardom, he had never felt comfortable with adulation, no matter how restrained.

He noted that Giselle Dupont, Searching Singles's other representative, was away from her desk.

They dumped their assortment of shopping bags and parcels on the floor of Becky's office. Though to call it an office was stretching it. It was really just the back third of the place sectioned off by a shoulder-high partition. Shoulder high on Rebecca; that was—on Zach the so-called wall didn't even reach his chest. He supposed an illusion of privacy was all Becky had wanted to achieve.

Being the kind of person who liked to have her finger on the pulse, so to speak, the ability to see and hear what went on in front would probably be even more important to her than executive seclusion.

While Rebecca quickly checked her phone messages and e-mail, Zach brazenly snooped here and there and eventually picked up the photo she kept on her desk. It showed her with husband Dale and twin sons Zachary and Dale, Jr. Both were grown men now; the picture was a decade out of date. But they were still as close-knit a family unit as they'd ever been.

Zach, though always made to feel like a part of that unit, had felt like an outsider nevertheless. "I always envied you," he quietly admitted when Becky came to look at the photo with him. "But these days..."

His little smile grew abashed as emotions that were still too new, and too immense to be taken for granted, roughened his voice to a husky whisper. "These days I can almost believe..."

He couldn't say any more, but knew that Becky understood. "You love that little girl, don't you?" she stated rather than asked.

Zach nodded, his eyes still on the picture in his hand, but seeing Nicole's image there, instead. "Yeah. I do."

"And the mom?"

The mom. Monica. The woman whose image was never far from his mind's eye and thoughts of whom could raise his pulse rate more effectively than three laps around his airfield.

Zach set down the picture. He couldn't bring himself to resent his sister's probing since, in a way, he had led up to it himself.

"She's great," he said, knowing full well that his answer didn't even begin to describe what Monica Griffith made him feel, but unwilling to be any more specific, even to someone as near and dear as Becky. "Like I told you, we've become friends. Good friends."

"Right." With a glance that made it clear to Zach that she was very good at reading between the lines, Rebecca changed direction. "Any sign of the ex?"

"Nope." Zach straightened the picture and stepped back. "I'd love to get my hands on him, though."

"Really." Becky's brows arched as she dug in her purse for a lipstick. "And do what?"

"Commit mayhem, sister, dear." Zach watched her apply lipstick with barely leashed impatience, and added, "Just as I'm going to do to you if you don't take me out and feed me. I'm starved."

* * *

Over lunch, Zach outlined some of Nicole's latest accomplishments. "She does incredible drawings," he bragged, oblivious to the fact that he sounded like a proud father. Or that his sister's eyes were glazing over.

"She knows the alphabet, can write all of our names. Monica's outstanding with her. They have lesson periods every day. And on the days Monica's in the office, she comes along, of course, and fools around on the old type-writer there."

"You ought to get her a computer."

"I've thought about it."

"Then do it. Get her one of those special ones for kids. They're wonderful learning tools. We'll pick one up this afternoon," she concluded, correctly taking Zach's agreement for granted.

Their salads came and for a few minutes, they ate in silence. Rebecca took a sip of water. "So has she got the puppy yet?"

"Charlie? No, not yet. Not in the house." Zach added salt and pepper to his greens. "We figure in another week or so."

"Charlie," Rebecca said. "And who came up with that name?"

"She did."

"She who? Monica?"

"Nicole."

"Nicole?" Becky repeated incredulously. "I thought she didn't speak."

"She didn't." Zach chewed a mouthful of his Cobb salad with a show of enjoyment that stemmed as much from confounding his sister and the sweet memory of Nicky's surprising first word as from the taste of the food. "I guess she wanted that puppy pretty bad."

"Bad enough to speak," Becky remarked in a tone of amazement, and shook her head. "Incredible."

"Yeah, isn't it?" Zach met his sister's pensive gaze and, recalling the moment when Nicky had made that first sound, said that first word, could feel his throat close up all over again. He drank some water, which helped some, not a lot.

"And now?" Becky prompted. "She talks?"

"No." He tore off a piece of crusty sourdough, but didn't carry it to his lips. He was thinking how very much Monica had hoped that, once started, Nicky would forever put silence behind her. Hell, so had he. "The doctor thinks she could, but that she simply doesn't feel it necessary to make the effort because all of us are so willing to understand her without words."

"So what's the answer? Ignoring her?"

"Probably." Zach's grin was rueful. "Not that any of us are about to do that. Poor little thing's had enough emotional turmoil dished out to her. Neither Monica nor I are willing to give her any more. No…" He sighed. "We wait and we hope, that's all."

"That's got to be hard." Becky patted her brother's hand. "But at least you know now that she's capa—"

She abruptly interrupted herself with an incredulous, "I don't believe it," as her attention was snagged by something beyond Zach's shoulder.

"What?" With a frown, Zach started to turn.

"Don't." Becky forestalled him, tightening her fingers around the hand she'd just leaned over to touch. "She saw me," she said with a sudden forced smile, releasing Zach's hand to raise hers in a greeting.

"Who?"

Becky, pointedly busy for a few moments with her own salad, didn't look up. "Dora. She must've just come in. She's in a booth, facing me."

"So? You did say she should go to lunch when Giselle got back." Though puzzled, Zach finally put the piece of bread he'd been holding into this mouth.

"She's with a man," Becky said. "And he's not a client."

Zach speared an anemic cherry tomato. "Good for her."

"I don't think so." Becky snuck another peek before turning troubled eyes on her brother. "Remember the man I called you about? The balding, spiffy dresser asking about Monica?"

She held his gaze, silent, while Zach leaped to the correct conclusion and nearly choked in the process.

"Richard Sinclair?"

"None other."

"With Dora?" Zach twisted around—to hell with discretion—and took a look for himself. A good look. He saw Dora studying the menu with what appeared to be complete absorption, but might well have been her way of avoiding further eye contact with Rebecca.

As to Sinclair, the man's back was toward him—wide shoulders in a well-cut suit jacket. And the back of a head that sported a tanned and shiny expanse of scalp above a long fringe of reddish hair tied back in a skimpy ponytail.

Well, well, Zach thought with seething contempt. *So that's the big man who gets off on pushing women and children around.*

It took every bit of self-control for him to stay put, to not march over there, haul the smarmy so-and-so out of the booth and flatten him.

He jerked back around and glared at Rebecca. "What would he want with her?" he demanded. "What does she know?"

"About you and..." Becky frowned. "Why, nothing. And I don't think she even worked the day he came into the office.

"Maybe it's just coincidence," she added with more hope than conviction.

"Oh, come on," Zach scoffed. "Next you'll tell me he's wooing the woman for her money and her looks."

Zach realized that his outrage—that a cretin like Sinclair should be free to dine in fancy restaurants while his ex-wife and child had to hide like fugitives—was making him sarcastic. And unfair.

He was glad Becky dismissed his insensitive comment with a roll of her eyes and an impatient, "I'm only saying that whatever *he* might think to the contrary, Dora knows nothing. Good grief, Zach, she only met Monica once and that's the day she flew in for the Brides thing."

"Was Nicky with her?"

"Well, yes. Of course. And Monica's mother. Carla..." She waved a hand, dismissing an obviously elusive last name. "I sent Dora to meet their plane and drive them to the hotel."

"Great." Zach brooded. There was no doubt in his mind that the man was pumping Dora for information. "So she's the one drove them to that fleabag you booked them into?"

"The Greenbriar is no fleabag," Becky objected. "It's clean, the location was convenient, and the rates met Monica's budget. And, yes, Dora drove them there."

"Which meant they chatted, introductions were made, and Dora found out that Carla Romanov lives in Kodiak."

"Maybe." Becky pushed away her plate; food had lost its appeal. "But not necessarily. Monica's reserved at the best of times, which these definitely aren't."

"True." Zach refused the waiter's offer of coffee and when Becky did the same, asked for the check. He was thinking that given her circumstances, Monica would have been the last person to volunteer anything about herself. He could only hope that Carla had been circumspect, too.

"How about at that reception?" he asked, still uneasy. "I don't recall seeing Dora there, but—"

"Another flu victim," Rebecca said. "Which was why I needed Monica there so badly. And because Giselle had a family thing she couldn't get out of."

"Okay." Zach sighed. He figured he had no choice but to believe that Dora had no way of knowing he was in any way involved. Which meant Monica and Nicky were safe. At least for now.

"Let's get out of here," he said to Becky, dropping a twenty onto the check as he rose. "Before I give in to the urge to go over there and punch the guy's lights out. Strictly on principle.''

They did the rest of Zach's errands, but without the pleasure they'd taken in the chore just that morning. Later, back in Becky's cubicle of an office to pick up the purchases they'd made that morning, they were silent; neither felt much like talking.

From across the partition, the other two women could be heard as they spoke on the telephone to what were obviously prospective clients. Every word of their sales pitch could be clearly understood.

Zach, overhearing, was peripherally intrigued by how differently each woman handled her call when suddenly it hit him. ''That's it!''

He motioned. ''Listen.''

Though visibly bewildered, Becky did as he asked. ''You mean, their sales pitch?'' she asked after a moment or two.

''No, no.'' Zach gestured impatiently. ''I mean that we can hear every word they're saying.''

When she continued to look blank, he sighed. ''If we can hear them, they can hear us. Or, more to the point, they can hear *you*. On the phone, talking with me. About…whatever.''

''Oh, boy.'' Catching on, Becky expelled a long and noisy breath. ''Up until this noon I'd have said, So what? I've got no secrets. But now…''

She considered a moment, and then, with sudden resolve, drew herself erect. ''We're gonna settle this thing right now.''

Before Zach could stop her, she was marching over to Dora's desk, only to return moments later with Dora in tow. Zach didn't need to see the woman's pained expression or hear what she had to say to know that Dora had sung for Richard Sinclair like the proverbial canary….

Meanwhile, back on Kodiak Island, Monica was in the Windemeer office. She had just about finished proofing the layouts for next year's advertising brochures. She had rediscovered her love—and talent—for art and promotion and had eagerly offered to take charge of that side of Windemeer Charters in addition to doing the all-around clerical chores her predecessor had dealt with.

In the process, she had learned a great deal about Zach's charter operation, as well as the man himself, and could only marvel at his versatility. Not only was Zach the consummate businessman, bush pilot, hunting guide, et cetera, et cetera, it seemed he had picked up a law degree at some point in his checkered past.

"Becky's fault," he'd reluctantly told her the day she'd asked him about it. She recalled the conversation perfectly, because he so rarely seemed to allow anyone a glimpse of himself, of who he had been.

"She meant it to be my continuing therapy," he had quipped, though with unmistakable gratitude and affection for his sister, and more than a hint of self-loathing for the sorry wreck he'd been at that time of his life. "After…Maddy. And the breakup of my marriage. After getting kicked out of the NBA and spending months at Betty Ford. And even more months with a shrink."

He looked away, but not before Monica had glimpsed the tortured expression in his eyes.

"It's not easy," he said, almost as though to himself," to regain this thing called self-respect. Or to learn to forgive yourself. To *like* yourself. You see—"

He glanced at Monica, and the pain she saw almost broke her heart. "I needed them to punish me. To lock me up. To cut off my hands, cut out my heart. And when they didn't, when they *wouldn't*, it seemed only right that I take care of it myself."

He laughed, a dry, bitter sound that was as far removed from mirth as anything could be. "But they wouldn't let me do that, either. Becky, the doctors, the shrink. They forced me to confront it all, to 'deal with it'—don't you just love that expression? *Deal with it. Be a man.* Get on with your life. That's another good one!''

Another mirthless chuckle shook Zach's chest. "My *life*. As though I wanted it! It was a mess! And it took quite a while to get it, and myself, straightened out. I did it for Maddy because one day it dawned on me that the only chance I had of becoming someone I could live with, was to live the kind of life I would have wanted Maddy to live—responsibly, unselfishly, soberly. And with honor. To do some good. To right some wrongs even though it would never be possible for me to right the wrong that I had committed.''

He shrugged, not carelessly, but with self-deprecation. "I studied law.''

"And?'' Monica prompted when he said no more but merely stared out the window.

He glanced at her, but Monica could tell he didn't really see her. "I found that that wasn't the answer, either. Mostly because I still didn't really get it.''

"Get it?'' Monica didn't understand. She frowned. "Get what?''

Zach straightened, his eyes sharply in focus. "What really counts. Which is *people*. I took on *issues*. More specifically, environmental issues. I argued for sanity and restraint on both sides, tried to help strike a balance between those who depend on logging for their livelihoods and those who see every tree that's felled as an irreplaceable loss. I found out the hard way that my refusal to align myself completely with one side or the other made me a not-very-popular man with either faction.''

"What happened?'' Monica asked because Zach's grim expression made it clear that something had. Something not very pleasant. But nothing could have prepared her for his answer.

"My house burned down.''

Monica gasped. "But... Who...''

Zach had shrugged, as though uncaring. But the way

he'd glanced away from Monica and pinched the bridge of his nose showed that he had cared, *still* cared, very much.

"It could have been someone from either side," he said. "Or maybe just one of those fluky hands life likes to deal us. I decided not to wait around and find out."

"You came to Alaska," Monica said. A statement, not a question.

Which Zach affirmed and elaborated on. "And I haven't practiced law since."

"Ah, but I happen to know that you have. And pro bono, at that." Monica had wiggled the piece of correspondence he'd given her to file, the one that had precipitated the conversation in the first place.

He'd brusquely waved it away. "Small stuff..."

"*People* stuff," Monica had countered. Whereupon Zach, muttering something about having things to do, had simply stalked off.

Neither of them had alluded to that conversation again. But Monica, who hoarded like a miser every little bit of himself that Zach, wittingly or unwittingly, revealed in the course of their time together, came to find out that his "people projects" were numerous and far-reaching. Only one of them was the yearly, all-expenses-paid, two-week camping and fishing experience he provided for needy children from all over the United States.

And through it all, she became increasingly convinced that if ever she should feel confident enough to fall in love again, Zacharius Robinson would be the man of her choice.

All the terrible things he had both suffered and committed in his past had, in her opinion, been more than atoned for while, at the same time, turning him into that rare thing—rare in Monica's experience, at least—a modest man. Self-effacing. Unassuming. Yet at ease with himself, and exuding a natural air of authority that she, on first acquaintance that evening at the North Star Hotel, had mistaken for arrogance.

How far they had come since that night, she mused, staring down at the brochures she had created. All of them. But mostly she and Nicole. They'd found a haven here at Windemeer. A place to belong. A…family. A family that included not just Zach, but Ada, and Mitch. Even Deke and that endearingly obnoxious Australian.

But always most importantly—Zach.

He had called last night to say that Becky had agreed to help him with the shopping and that he'd likely be home around noon tomorrow. He'd be surprised by how far she'd gotten with these layouts, Monica thought, missing him.

Missing him. She looked up. Blinked. She'd gotten so used to having him around, quietly, steadfastly going about his business while she went about hers at her own desk across the room that it was kind of scary, the realization that she really hated having him gone.

Oh, Zach. Indulging herself for a moment, Monica leaned back in the chair and conjured up his face. His presence. As it invariably did when he was near her in person, her pulse sped up.

And her heart expanded with emotions that were as exhilarating as they were frightening. As exciting as they were depressing. The dichotomy was as inevitable as her situation was unsure.

For how could she dare give in to those feelings, attractions, and dreams when the threat, the all-pervading fear, of discovery, and of losing Nicky, was such a constant reality?

How could she dare let herself give in to the longings of her young and healthy body, and to the even stronger yearnings of her bruised and battered heart when *uncertainty was the only certainty she could see in her future?

If only…

Useless wishful thinking was what Zach considered

those words. Yet Monica thought them often at times like this, times of reflection when her defenses were at an ebb and when it seemed that happiness would forever remain out of reach.

Happiness. And Zach. Two things which seemed equally unattainable. And which, somewhere along the line, had become synonymous for Monica.

As they had for Nicky.

Poor Nicky. With a heavy sigh, Monica contemplated both the wonder and the heartbreak of her daughter's attachment to their benefactor. The wonder, because by allowing herself to trust and love this man, Nicole had crossed a mountainous emotional hurdle.

The heartbreak would occur for both, the child and the man, when it came time for them to part.

Even this short trip of Zach's had caused Nicole anxiety and anguish. The upside of that anguish was that it had led to another breakthrough—tears.

At bedtime last night, when Zach wasn't there to read *Winnie-The-Pooh*, Nicole had sat in her bed and cried.

Monica could have wept then, too. Only in her case the tears would have been tears of joy. Every scrap of progress, however minuscule it might seem to an outsider, represented a major triumph as far as Monica was concerned. More, it served as justification for her stubborn conviction that, with time and patience, as well as sufficient motivation, Nicole could and would be as normal as any other child.

With a twist of her body, Monica swiveled her chair so that she faced Zach's desk again and, next to it, the little work area Zach had created for Nicky. Nicole wasn't there this morning. With Zach away, she had chosen to go with Ada to visit the pups in the barn rather than bang away at the old typewriter and spin the dial of the defunct, old-fashioned black phone.

Many times she—Monica—and Zach had observed Nicole having silent conversations on it with imaginary callers. Today, as at those other times, Monica wondered rather sadly who those callers might be.

"Hel-lo, gorgeous!"

Torn out of her reverie by this loud, male greeting, Monica swung around with a hand to her throat. She stared, unnerved, into blue eyes that were full of the devil.

"Sorry, love," their owner said, not looking a bit repentant. "Didn't mean to startle you then!"

But, of course, he had—Roger Creswell, the Australian. Monica suspected he got a kick out of unsettling her any way he could. If not with his teasing and easy charm, or his outrageous flirtation, then by simply sneaking up on her the way he'd just done.

He bent to her, straight white teeth a startling contrast to the deeply tanned skin of his undeniably handsome face. His eyes danced. "Sleeping on the job when the boss is away, hmm?"

"I was not," she replied tartly. "Ever hear of knocking before coming in, *mate?*"

"On the door of a business office? Not likely." He perched on the edge of her desk, arms crossed, while the wattage of his grin increased. "And the word is 'mate.' He pronounced it "moit." "Better keep working on the accent."

"I'll give it top priority." Her poise recovered, and because she wanted to laugh but didn't want to give him the satisfaction, she returned her attention to the layout. "Here, give me your valued opinion. Is, and I quote, 'Windemeer's excellent staff of pilots and guides will guarantee an unforgettable wilderness experience in America's last frontier' unquote, overstating it?"

"Well…" Roger pursed his lips, tapping his chin with eyes turned ceilingward as if giving the question serious consideration. "Maybe."

He looked back at Monica and wiggled his brows. "Unless, of course, you're referring to me with that excellent pilot and guide bit."

"Oh, for heaven's sake!" Exasperated, Monica gathered up the layout and stuffed it into a folder. "I must've gone momentarily insane, thinking I could get you to say one serious word."

She stuck the folder into a drawer and slammed it. "So what do you want, *Crocodile Dundee?*"

"Why, a serious word, of course." Roger, as aware of the situation with Monica and Nicole, and as protective of them as everyone else on Windemeer, wasn't nearly as callous as he liked to make himself out to be. And Monica knew that, of course. The man might be an incorrigible charmer and a cut-up, but he adored Nicole and was devoted to Zach.

"Oh?" In the face of Roger's uncharacteristically quick about-face, Monica tensed. It generally took several pointed barbs to get him to get down to anything but monkey business. "What's the matter?"

"Got a telephone call," he said, inspecting his nails and swinging his foot. "About a charter."

"At the hangar?" Charters were always booked through the office. In season, which this was not. Still, Zach had told her they would do emergency flights when possible. Mercy flights, that sort of thing.

But those, too, were arranged through the office, not the shop. At least, she'd thought they were. "That's odd," she said. "Isn't it?"

"Yup." The eyes that looked at her now weren't laughing. Not even close. "And it gets odder. Bloke who called said he knew the boss was away and would I be interested in making a quick five hundred for myself, flying him here from Seldovia."

"Here?"

"To Kodiak."

"And you think what?" Though the thought that it was Richard leaped instantly to mind, Monica refused to give in to such paranoid thinking. It had been weeks since he had showed up at Zach's sister's business. And Rebecca hadn't told him a thing. He'd have been here by now, if he'd traced them some other way. "That he was a crook?"

"Well, he wasn't Father O'Malley coming home to the parish, I can tell you that much for sure."

"Right." Monica bit her lip, choking back butterflies. "So what did you say?"

"What do you think I said?" Roger looked insulted. "Get lost, or words to that effect. I don't work for money under the table. I'm straight with the boss, one hundred percent."

"Of course. I didn't mean to imply…"

"Yeah, yeah." Dismissing her attempt to apologize with a brusque wave of the hand, Roger got off the desk and sauntered to the door. "I also told him to call Jefferson, Inc."

For just an instant, Monica didn't get it. But then a light went on and she clapped a hand to her mouth, laughing. "You didn't."

Jefferson, Inc., was, strictly speaking, one of Windemeer Charters's competitors. Except that Sam Jefferson, owner and pilot, ran a very slipshod operation that was constantly running afoul of the F.A.A. "Oh, Roger, you're terrible."

"Too right." Roger blew her a kiss before closing the door. "It's why all you sheilas adore me."

The ringing of the phone coincided with his exit line. Still chuckling, Monica picked up the receiver. "Windemeer Charters."

"You sound happy." It was Zach. His mellow baritone was unmistakable and never failed to send her pulse into overdrive.

"Roger just left."

"Good ol' Roge." A little bite crept into the mellowness.

Monica flattered herself that Zach might be jealous. "He can be a scoundrel," she admitted, not above fanning the flame just a bit. Even if the flame wasn't really lit. "But," her conscience immediately made her add, "the reason he came into the office was that he'd had a rather peculiar phone call.''

''Oh?'' Zach's tone, to Monica, seemed suddenly to reverberate with tension. ''Who from? Did he say?''

''Well...'' Monica quickly reiterated what Roger had told her.

And gasped, her hand to her throat, when Zach grimly said, ''That does it.'' Quickly summing up for her the situation in Anchorage, he ended with a curt, ''I'm flying home tonight.''

Chapter Eight

One day passed, two days, a week. Nicole was confined to the house unless accompanied by an adult. An adult other than Monica, that is. Zach considered her as much at risk from Richard Sinclair as the little girl.

Rebecca telephoned to say that Sinclair had not been seen or heard from again at the Anchorage end.

"Dora swears that now she knows who and what he is, she wouldn't see him again if he were the last man on earth."

"Unfortunately," Zach said sourly, "that's a bit like shutting the barn door after the cattle got out."

"I know. But she feels terrible...."

They all felt terrible. Confined. Worried. On edge. And, in Monica's case, scared. Though she admitted that only to herself. Zach's constant proximity was pleasure and torture combined. She could practically feel her nerves shredding, one by one.

Fear was making her restless and impatient. She found it difficult to concentrate on any given task. She wondered whatever had possessed her to think it would be fun to sew

Halloween costumes. Which was what she was doing at her mother's house in Kodiak since there was no sewing machine at Windemeer.

Muttering to herself about costumes from hell, Monica ripped out yet another seam and swore all those dots were making her eyes spin like gyros. No wonder she had a headache.

And she wished Richard Sinclair would just make his move and get it over with.

Not that she considered for even a moment the eventuality of his succeeding to get to her or Nicole; Zach had taken too many precautions for there to be any chance of that. No, the scenario she envisioned and prayed for, was that the man would pounce, get nabbed, and leave her free to finally get on with her life.

The trouble was, of course, that it would mean she'd be moving on. After all, without danger lurking in the form of Richard Sinclair and his schemes, there would be no reason whatever for her and Nicole to stay at Windemeer.

Unless she were to marry Zach. He had, after all, asked her to. And she, in her heart of hearts, had long since admitted to herself that she would gladly say yes. *If only...*

Those words again. Those useless words. Yet appropriate, darn it! *If only he loved her!* There! She'd said it!

Yes, but what did that accomplish? The man hasn't made one single move in your direction since that night on the porch. Or done anything else that could even remotely be interpreted as a romantic gesture.

That doesn't mean he won't.

Yeah, right.

"Ouch." Monica sucked on the finger she'd just pricked with a pin and told herself to keep her mind on her work.

But her mind wouldn't listen, it was too busy whispering. Prodding...

You don't want a man, remember? A man got you into this mess in the first place.

Yes, but Zach's different.

Ha!
He's good.
He's a man.
And kind.
He's a man.
I love him.
Silence. And then, *You're a fool!*

"Don't I know it," Monica snapped out loud. Impatient with herself and her nonsensical thoughts, she snatched a tissue out of the box and wrapped it around her finger. She blamed the fact that her hands were shaking on nerves and forced herself to concentrate on the bulky seam she had repinned. It was part of the dratted Dalmatian's tail and getting it back under the pressure foot of her mother's old Singer was quite a challenge.

There. Satisfied that it was finally in place and passably straight, Monica applied pressure with her knee and fed the fabric along as the needle bobbed up and down, up and—

"Damn it!"

"Now, Monica..." Carla came into the room in time to hear her daughter's uncharacteristic loss of temper.

Monica slumped. She mentally counted to ten to get hold of herself. "That's the second time the darned needle broke."

"Here. Let me." Carla nudged her off the chair. "Go take a break. I'll sew for a while."

"I hate this costume."

"No, you don't." Carla dislodged the material as Monica, glad to surrender the project for a while, stretched the stiffness out of her back. "Look how cute Nicky's turned out."

And it had, Monica admitted, admiring it where it hung on the hanger.

"It's going to be such fun to have the three of you all look the same." Carla, familiar with her machine, had made short work of replacing the needle and was deftly rethreading it. She looked at the bulky seam. "I think if we trimmed a bit here, and here…"

Monica was happy to leave her to it. "What's Nicky up to?"

"Would you believe she's napping?"

"No, but as cranky as she's been lately, I won't look that gift horse in the mouth." Nicole, no doubt picking up on the tension that was putting the adults' nerves on edge, had been particularly fractious lately. "Think I'll make some coffee."

"I already did." The machine whirred as Carla sewed the now-trimmed seam with no apparent difficulty. "Zach came a bit ago."

"Oh?" Monica's lethargy vanished and there was a spring in her step as she headed for the door. "You should've said something sooner."

His presence filled her mother's small kitchen. Somehow, at Windemeer, she no longer noticed what a large man he was. Tall and muscular—a grizzled former athlete still very much in shape. And attractive?

Oh, yes. He was that. At least to Monica. Increasingly, unfortunately, nerve-wrackingly so.

So much so that when he turned from the window at the sound of her entering and their eyes met, an achy sort of rush closed her throat. She couldn't speak. Couldn't say hello as all the silly longings she'd dwelled on upstairs reverberated through her heart.

I love you, Zach.

She wondered what he'd do if she said those words out loud. Would he kiss her? She wanted him to.…

Zach couldn't move, nor could he look away. Something, some inner glow, some magical light in Monica's eyes kept him rooted where he stood, spellbound, hardly daring to breathe for fear of shattering the moment.

Kiss me, Zach.

Had she spoken? Or had all those nights he'd lain sleepless with frustrated desire finally robbed him of his good sense?

The coffeemaker gurgled and hissed out a shot of steam. Monica released the doorknob and the door clicked shut.

They were alone. Together. And the air between them as they gazed into each other's eyes was charged with the kind of tension that could only exist when a man and woman wanted. Desired. Loved...

Did Monica move toward him? Or was it Zach who took those two long steps that brought them within inches of each other? Neither of them knew, nor cared. All that mattered was reflected in their eyes as they clung, searched, approved, and as their hands reached out to each other. And...touched.

How, Monica wondered dimly while the flames in Zach's eyes ignited the banked fires in all her secret places, how could she ever have thought he didn't care?

He shifted his gaze to her lips, making them tingle with anticipation. He said, "I've wanted to kiss you for such a long time."

"And I... I've been wishing you would," Monica admitted on a soft exhalation that parted her lips in that instant before his possession.

His kiss was hard, hot. And swift. He raised his head, searched her face. "Are you sure?"

Monica blinked up at him. "Sure about what?"

"About this." He kissed her again, deeply this time. Passionately. Carnally. With his tongue, with his teeth, while his hands roamed and fondled, intimately. Possessively.

And, to Monica, so very, very excitingly. "Oh, yes," she murmured, letting her head fall back in abandon as Zach trailed hot, open-mouthed kisses along her jaw, down her throat. "Oh, please, yes..."

She was quivering, kissing him back, clinging to him, her body a mass of sensations that were urging her toward the kind of fulfillment she only dimly realized would be impossible for them to achieve right here and right now.

Which only added fuel and urgency to her response. If this was all she could have for the moment, then let it be everything she'd ever dreamed of.

"Oh, Zach," she whispered. "More, more…"

And Zach's ardor took wing. He let go of restraint, knocked down all the barriers he'd so carefully erected around his heart and reached for the stars.

They were both breathless and flushed when at last they drew apart. Not much. Just enough so that Zach could look into Monica's slumberous eyes. "Oh, my darling girl," he whispered, for what he saw made his hopes soar right along with his heart. She was his. She might not know it yet, but she was his.

"Marry me," he whispered, baring his need to her. His feelings, his heart. "We're good together, you and I. You feel it, too, don't you? Tell me it isn't just me…"

"It isn't just you," Monica whispered before melting into him once more.

"Then marry me," he urged when the need for air made them reluctantly draw apart once again. "We're already a family, you, me. And Nicky. I love that little girl. And you…"

He kissed her. "I can't look at you without wanting you. In my arms, in my life. In my bed.

"Feel," he whispered huskily, tugging her closer, adjusting his stance until they were as intimately aligned as a man and a woman could be. "Feel how much you make me want you…."

Want you… Want you… Want…

It wasn't the word she needed to hear, *longed* to hear, this word that was going around and around in her brain and made sanity return in a chilling rush. Would she ever hear it from this man to whom she had so foolishly lost her heart?

She searched his eyes, so bright, so hot with...*desire*.
And thought, *Want* isn't enough. Not nearly enough.

Monica shuddered, suddenly cold. She'd been there,
she'd been in a marriage without love. She'd done that.
And even though she knew that Zach Robinson in no way
resembled Richard Sinclair, she'd never enter into a love-
less marriage again.

"Oh, Zach..." Immeasurably weary and discouraged,
she let her forehead drop against Zach's shoulder and wondered how to say to him what she needed to.

As it turned out, she was spared from having to say
anything at all because Nicky, rubbing the sleep out of her
eyes, chose that moment to walk into the kitchen.

Zach and Monica immediately drew apart, both aware
that any change of the status quo, no matter whether good
or bad, was potentially traumatic to Nicole.

"Hi, sweetie." Monica was glad to let the simple chores
of motherhood restore her equilibrium and put some distance between herself and Zach. She scooped Nicky up
and sat down with her, rocking her child and savoring the
sweet smell of her as Nicole nestled against her and slowly
came fully awake.

Monica carefully avoided looking at Zach, but felt his
indulgent gaze like a physical touch.

He enjoys seeing me like this, she thought with a flash
of resentment. *Madonna with child or some such male fan-
tasy. Or maybe he thinks I'm everything his party-girl wife
was not.*

Well, I need more than that. And such was her disillu-
sionment that, when Zach came to gently take Nicky off
her lap—as he had done countless times before—she
snapped at him. "Leave her. She's fine."

She could have wept when Nicky promptly slid off her
lap and into Zach's arms.

She pointedly looked away when Zach, swinging her
daughter high up in the air, tried to catch her eye with a

wry, adult-to-adult glance that clearly was meant to say, "Kids. Go figure…"

She didn't need him to explain her own child to her, she thought, knowing she was being peevish and unfair. In fact, she didn't need him at all.

It wasn't until much later, back at Windemeer, that Monica and Zach were once more alone. He caught her in the hall, after reading Nicole her bedtime story while Monica had tidied the bathroom after Nicky's bath. By then, Monica's emotions had returned to a more reasonable state, but her heartache had only grown worse and she really didn't feel up to another face-off with Zach.

"She's asleep," he whispered, snagging Monica's hand and sweeping her into an embrace with a lazy, "Now where were we this afternoon, before we were so rudely interrupted?"

Because it would have been so very easy to succumb, and because at his touch, her stupid heartbeat lurched, Monica marshaled every defense she had by calling to mind her earlier feelings of disappointment. She went rigid as a board. "Don't."

She pushed him away by flattening both palms against his chest and was further incensed by the knowledge that only Zach's surprise at her—to him, unexpected—reaction had made him release her.

"I don't want this," she said, turning away and putting a hand to her forehead where a very real headache was adding to her misery.

"Come again?" Zach sounded puzzled.

"You heard me." As a child, her mother had always threatened Monica with lightning strikes from the sky if she lied. And so, half expecting a thunderbolt to smite her, she crossed her fingers. "I don't want you…to touch me. That way."

It seemed like forever before Zach spoke. But the tension between them was potent enough to ignite an electrical storm. "What about this afternoon?" he finally asked. His tone was neutral; it betrayed nothing of what he felt.

Which put her at a disadvantage, but Monica didn't have the courage to turn around for a look at his face. "I..." She nervously cleared her throat. "It was a mistake."

"A *mistake?*" Just like that, neutrality gave way to incredulity. Zach stepped in front of her, tried unsuccessfully to capture her chin and raise her face. "Damn it, Monica, you look me in the eye and say that."

She couldn't. Bad enough she had said it once. But she also couldn't tell him what had brought her to this. Not without making herself completely vulnerable to him, not without risking rejection.

Or, much worse, making herself into an object of pity.

She'd rather he call her fickle, Monica thought. Only to immediately add, No, she wouldn't. Feeling utterly wretched, she eluded his touch and kept her eyes averted. "I'm sorry, Zach."

It was the apology that sent Zach over the edge.

"You're *sorry?*" Disappointment, hurt and frustration making him rough, he shoved her back against the wall and pinned her with his body. "About this?"

He kissed her, kissed her hard. His teeth scraped hers and drew blood on her lips. The taste of it rather than the pummeling her fists gave his shoulders instantly restored his reason. What in the *hell* was he doing? He jerked away, breathing hard, and they stared at each other. Zach saw fear in Monica's eyes. Fear of him.

"Oh, Lord. Monica..." He was sick with self-disgust. "Baby, I—"

"Don't," Monica said. "Please."

But it was her pallor and her haunted expression that silenced him, not the words. And it was shame for his own caveman tactics that made him turn on his heel and walk away.

Gradually, over the next few days, tensions eased. If not between Monica and Zach, then at least as far as Richard

Sinclair was concerned. As another week went by without incident, guards were lowered, restrictions relaxed.

Nicole, with Charlie by her side, was allowed to venture out of doors again, though no farther than the hangar, the barn, or Mitch's cottage.

Charlie's sire, Zeus, had attached himself to Nicole soon after the runt of his mate's litter went to live with her at the big house. No one could figure out what his motives were; concern for his offspring being highly unlikely. Cookies and other morsels from Nicole seemed more plausible incentives since even a proud and dignified malamute like Zeus was not above accepting treats.

But it was Mitch's opinion that the dog sensed Nicole's inherent vulnerability and had simply appointed himself her protector.

Whatever, Zach mused, watching the little girl and her canine entourage of two cross from the barn to the hangar. It made him feel a whole lot better, knowing the powerful dog was by her side.

He turned away from the window. Roger would willingly entertain the child with his colorful, if improbable tales of koala bears, emu and wallabies for as long as she cared to listen. All three of his men had taken to her, which was hardly surprising since he, himself, adored her, too.

Adored her, loved her mother. Now what could be more simple and straightforward than that?

Everything, it seemed.

With a dark glance in the direction of Monica, diligently at work at the computer, Zach stalked to his desk and sat down. He shuffled papers and forced himself to look as busy and involved as Monica seemed to be.

But his mind was far from the workings of Windemeer Charters. It kept returning to the Romanovs' kitchen and the interlude he'd shared there with Monica while Carla sewed and Nicole took her nap.

And for the hundredth time or more asked himself, How

could it all have gone so wrong? What had he misinterpreted?

Not Monica's response to his lovemaking. No way. No how. He was no green youth; he knew the difference between the genuine article and pretense.

Monica's desire that afternoon had matched his. She had trembled, as he had. Ached, as he had. And she had wanted him as desperately as he had wanted her. It had been there in the way she clung to him, rocked with him hip to hip while their tongues did the dance that their bodies were denied by time, by place, by circumstance. It had been there.

But where had it gone? And why? What the hell had she meant, saying it was all a mistake?

Thoroughly depressed, Zach pressed thumb and forefinger into the corners of his eyes. They'd been acting like polite strangers since that day and he wished to God he knew how to get beyond that without forfeiting any more of his pride.

Pride. It was all he had left. And not very much of that. Because in spite of calling himself an old fool and worse, he hadn't been able to keep himself from approaching her, to make an attempt at a dialogue to clear the air, and to try to apologize for his Neanderthal behavior.

And each time she had shoved another piece of his pride down his throat by turning away with a strained, "Please, Zach, I wish you'd just forget it."

Not that she was callous. He could see, as he watched her walk up to his desk, that she was hurting as badly as he was. Her eyes were huge. They looked like bruises in a face as pale as milk. Her dress hung shapelessly from her shoulders. She had visibly lost weight.

"You're working too hard," he said gruffly.

Monica bent to retrieve a file he hadn't even noticed had slid to the floor. "Not nearly hard enough to repay you for everything I owe."

"Everything you—" Goaded beyond endurance, Zach surged to his feet. "Damn it, Monica!"

"I'm sorry," she immediately said.

Which infuriated Zach even more. "Well, so am I," he snapped. "About a lot of things."

He wished he'd hung on to his temper the moment he saw her face grow paler still. And her bottom lip quiver before she flattened her mouth into a hard, straight line.

Chagrined, he blew out a breath. "Look. This is—"

"It's quite all right," Monica interrupted. She laid some letters on his desk. "These are for your signature before you leave the office."

He wanted to strangle her. He wanted to kiss her. But, most of all, he wanted to understand what was eating her. "Monica," he said, gentling his tone. "Talk to me. Please."

He came out from behind the desk and restrained her when she would have walked away. "Whatever it is, whatever I *said,* if you'll just tell me, I'm sure we—"

"I can't." *It's what you didn't say, Zach.* Her eyes met his and implored him to leave it alone. She drew a breath that was as shaky as her voice, but she squared her shoulders and said, "I hate to bring this up right now, but... Well, it's Halloween today and we need to be leaving for my mother's house pretty soon, Nicky and I. She wants you to go, too, of course."

"Of course." Zach compressed his lips and struggled to swallow the bitterness that had risen like bile into this throat. He'd struck out again. And another piece of pride had bitten the dust. He scowled to keep his injured feelings from showing. "The question is, what do *you* want?"

"What I want," Monica totally floored him by whispering, "is for us to be friends again." A sheen of moisture glazed her eyes. "The way we used to be."

"And you think that's possible?"

"No." Some tears spilled, streaking her cheeks as Monica shook her head. "I guess not. But maybe, for Nicky's sake—"

"Yeah," Zach cut in. Giving in to the need to touch her, he framed her face with his hands and gently wiped the tears away with his thumbs. "For Nicky's sake..."

"For once it's not pouring with rain, thank God," Carla Romanov said. She and her husband, Pete, a great bear of a man whose bushy beard covered most of his face, were out on the porch putting final touches on a huge, evil-faced, jack-o'-lantern perched atop a ladder draped by a sheet to make it look like a ghostly body when Monica and Zach followed Nicole up the porch steps.

"Just wait'll it gets dark and the candle's lit inside his head," Pete said to Nicole with a wink. "He'll really look scary then."

Nicole grinned back at the gentle giant. It had taken very little effort on his part to win her over. With his twinkling eyes and ready sense of fun, Pete Romanov was a man who had never met a stranger. Or been cowed by unresponsive silence. He simply kept right on talking and joking when, in the beginning, Nicole would just sit on her chair, or when she shrank back whenever he came near.

Until one day, to everyone's surprise but Pete's, she no longer shrank away. And even laughed out loud at his antics.

Watching the trusting way Nicky put her hand in her step-granddad's huge paw, Monica decided that maybe a move into town would no longer be traumatic for her little girl.

Because the way things were now, she really couldn't stay at Windemeer any longer. Zach was right—they couldn't go back. And yet there was nothing to go forward to, was there?

"Ada sent a pumpkin pie, Ma." She preceded her mother, who was holding the door, into the house and through to the kitchen. She set down the pie.

"Is something wrong between you and Zach?" Carla immediately asked.

"Wrong?" Monica slipped out of her jacket. "Why do you ask?"

Her mother shrugged and put the kettle on to boil. "Just a feeling."

"Oh. Well." Monica kept her eyes on the jacket she was carefully draping over the back of a chair. "Stress is getting to all of us, I guess."

"Hmm."

Monica turned to the pie. "Which is, uh, partly why I've been thinking that maybe Nicky and I could, you know, come stay here with you for a while."

Monica kept her eyes on her hands, taking the foil off the pie. Of course, her mother would be convinced now that something *was* wrong between Zach and herself, but that couldn't be helped. "If your invitation's still open."

"Well, of course, but—"

"Nicky's so much better," Monica said quickly. "In fact, Doc Koontz thinks she would really benefit from some instruction from someone other than me."

Which was not entirely a lie. On a recent visit Doc *had* indicated that down the road a ways some kind of special classes a couple of days a week could certainly be beneficial in helping Nicole fully recover her speech.

"Living here with you," Monica went on, "I wouldn't need to worry about driving her back and forth. Quite aside from the fact that I don't own a car, I really think we've been imposing on Zach way too long already."

"I never got the feeling that Zach considers what he's doing for Nicky and you an imposition, dear," her mother protested. "In fact, I'd say quite the contrary. Having the two of you at his place gives him..."

She shrugged. "Oh, I don't know, at least as much benefit as Nicole and you are getting out of being there. Maybe more. If I hadn't been convinced of that, I'd have insisted you leave there weeks ago."

Carla touched her daughter's shoulder, made her turn when she would have gone to put the pie on the sideboard. "Zach *loves* that child like his own," she said gently.

And drew back with an expression of shock when Monica promptly burst into tears with a choked, "Don't you think I know that?"

"Well, then?" Carla asked, at a loss. She took the pie out of Monica's hands and set it down.

"It's not enough," Monica whispered and buried her face in her hands. "I want him…to love…*meee*…"

"Aw, honey…" Tut-tutting, Carla put her arms around her daughter and led her to the table. "Come on now. Sit down and I'll make us some tea."

She bustled off to the stove where the kettle shrilled. Monica propped her elbows on the table and raked her hair off her face. She couldn't believe what she'd just said and fervently wished she hadn't. Even to someone as unjudgmental as her mother. Out loud it had sounded so…pathetic. Even petty. Almost as though she were jealous. Of her own daughter!

"Oh, Ma." She covered her eyes with a groan. "I didn't mean to fall apart like this, or sound the way I sounded. I…"

"You think I don't know that?" Carla put a steaming mug of mint tea within reach. "You've been under a terrible strain for months now, even years. Who wouldn't fall apart with all that?"

She gave Monica a hug combined with a little shake. "And where better to do it than in your mom's kitchen? Hmm?" She slid the mug closer. "Here. Drink and collect yourself and we'll talk."

Monica obediently took a sip, but couldn't relax. She kept glancing toward the door through which Zach was likely to appear at any moment. "Do I look like I've been crying?" she asked.

Carla handed her a tissue. "Blot your eyes and you'll

look fine." She sat down across from Monica. "I think you're wrong, you know."

Monica lowered the tissue. "About what?"

"About Zach." Carla lifted her own mug, blew on it, then set it back down. "A lot of women would kill to have a man look at them the way that man looks at you."

"Oh." Depressed, Monica wadded the tissue and dabbed once more at the corners of her eyes. "Looks like *that*, Mother, are simply *lust*," she said morosely. "And contrary to what you might have read in books, that's not the stuff of romance and happily-ever-after."

"Oh, really?" Carla's eyebrows arched.

"Yes," Monica said. "Really."

Neither Monica nor Zach was even remotely in the mood when it came time to put on the Dalmatian suits. The things were basically a jumpsuit with a tail. A snugly fitted hood with ears on top went over the head.

Carla delighted herself, Pete and Nicky by applying white makeup to their faces and black paint to the end of Zach and Monica's noses. The recipients of the "nose job" simply endured in silence.

Monica couldn't imagine ever thinking this was a cute idea.

Zach couldn't for the life of him figure out how he'd let himself get roped into this.

One look at Nicole's shining eyes and beaming face, however, reminded them both what it was all about.

And so they smiled, even laughed as they took turns answering the door and handing out treats with Nicky their ever-eager helper.

"Why, hello, Mr. President!" Monica laughingly beckoned to one of the fathers, hanging back while a score of witches, space men and Jasmine wannabes clambered up the Romanovs' porch steps demanding treats. The man was huddled into a black down jacket, his entire head covered by a rubbery Bill Clinton mask.

"Come on up," she invited, hoisting a plastic glass. "We've got hot spiced cider to warm up dedicated dads like you."

She shrugged when the man shook his head and shrunk back into the shadows.

"Bashful," she whispered to Nicole who, along with Zach, was dropping generous handfuls of candy into pillowcases, plastic pumpkins and paper sacks. "But that's his loss, right?"

As they had hoped, after about an hour of playing Lady Bountiful, Nicky felt brave enough to do some trick-or-treating of her own. So Monica and Zach bundled her and themselves into sweaters beneath their costumes and joined the fray.

Pete and Carla's house was in an older, quiet neighborhood that had recently experienced a renaissance of sorts in the form of young couples buying fix-up homes. As a consequence, there were lots of young children in the neighborhood which pleased the Romanovs greatly since crime tended not to be a problem in family oriented sections of a city.

The streets were packed with adults and children of all ages in costumes of every description, from fantastic to fanciful to makeshift. With lots of scary masks, to boot.

Looking around, Zach remarked, "Well, I don't feel quite so conspicuous anymore."

Monica swept him a glance. The strain of having to present a happy face in front of Nicole was beginning to wear on her nerves. And the fact that, dressed in that dopey costume Zach looked endearing and cuddly in a big, brawny man sort of way that was making her breath catch and her heart ache, was not helping her frame of mind.

"I guess you have to be a kid to look good in these things," she said a bit tartly.

Or have a figure like yours, Zach thought. And out loud said, "At least we're warm," with a purposely overdone leer at a nubile, but shivering Jasmine in skimpy harem finery.

"She should have worn a coat," Monica said.

"Spoken like a mother," said Zach.

"I guess that's because I am one."

"Yup." Zach sighed. "Can't fault you there." Which probably wouldn't have come out sounding like criticism if his own nerves weren't every bit as tightly wound as Monica's obviously were.

And so he wasn't really surprised when she immediately took offense, snapping, "And what is *that* supposed to mean?" in a hissing whisper over Nicky's head.

"That it might be refreshing to let yourself be a woman once in a while," he retorted in a muted growl, and matched her glare for glare.

If she were honest, Monica would have admitted that their mutedly heated exchange was making her feel alive again in a most delicious way. And, if asked, she would have bet that Zach's smoldering glares were an indication of a similar state of exhilaration.

Which was why, with their gazes locked in an unspoken promise of more to come, it was several moments before she became aware that Nicky was tugging on her hand and pointing, wanting to be free to join a group of kids going up the stairs to the door of the house in front of which they had stopped.

She immediately released the child with a pat of encouragement on her spotted little rump, but without taking her eyes off Zach's.

The moment Nicky was out of earshot, she drawled, "Why, because your hormones are raging and you need one in your bed?"

Now it was Zach who took offense. "Is that what you think I'm about with regard to you? Hormones?"

"Well, aren't you?"

"No! But, damn it, if that's what you think then I've obviously—"

"Excuse me, mister…" The hit-and-miss tenor of an adolescent boy whose voice was changing made Zach's head snap around.

"What!" he barked, annoyed to be interrupted just when he and Monica were on the brink of getting some vital issues out into the open.

"Is this your little girl?" To Zach and Monica's horror he pushed a silently weeping Nicole toward them. "I figured by the costumes that she would be. She was lost, I think. That man over there—" They all looked to where he pointed, just in time to see a man in a Bill Clinton mask quickly duck into the crowd. "Was talkin' to her. But I could see she was a-scared and crying, so I grabbed her by the hand and took her back to you."

"Thank God." Beside herself, Monica sank to her knees and clasped Nicky close. *How could you?* she furiously chastised herself. *How could you have been so involved in your stupid argument with Zach to forget about your child?*

Zach, though equally appalled at himself, snapped, "You stay here with them," to the youthful Good Samaritan before taking off after the guy in the mask. Having whoever it was twice lurk near the two females that meant the world to him was just one coincidence too many.

Besides, his gut told him that Clinton mask hid Richard Sinclair.

Unfortunately, the man was nowhere to be found, even though Zach ran a block in every direction. Knowing it was fruitless to search further, and reminding himself belatedly that he had left Monica and Nicky essentially defenseless, he hurried back to where he'd started from.

But only the youth was still there.

Chapter Nine

The boy had his back toward Zach. Zach, frantic because there was no sign of Nicky and Monica, looked in the direction the kid's attention was focused and saw that, up the road a ways, a patrol car with its lights flashing had pulled up to the curb. A small crowd milled around the trooper. But there, too, no Dalmatian costumes were to be seen. Nor anyone in a Bill Clinton mask. Two scruffy and belligerent teenagers were being lectured by the cop.

Dismissing the scene, Zach clamped a hand on the boy's shoulder and spun him around. "Where are they?"

The youth blinked, visibly frightened by the ferocity of Zach's tone and expression. Zach had long since torn the doggie hood off his head; sweat from running, and the fine mist that was shrouding everything in ghostly softness now, had plastered his hair to his temples and face. "Answer me," he growled, increasing the pressure on the boy's shoulder.

The youth swallowed. "Sh-she said to t-tell you t-they were g-going home," he stammered.

Zach bit off an oath and let the kid go so abruptly that

he staggered back a few steps. He would have turned and run, but Zach grabbed him by the arm with one hand while digging through an open side seam in his costume for some money in his pocket.

"Here." He came up with a twenty and pressed it into the kid's hand. "Thanks, and... I didn't mean to get rough."

"Hey, no problem." The kid beamed, fisting his hand around the money. "Thanks, mister," he called after Zach who had jogged off toward the Romanovs'.

He prayed that Monica and Nicole would be there. And was weak with relief, and then furious, when they were.

"What the *hell* were you thinking?" he snarled, after literally dragging Monica out of the kitchen into the hall for some privacy. "I tell you to stay put somewhere, you damned well stay put, do you hear me? Have you any idea how I felt when you weren't there?"

"It told the boy—"

"I *know* what you told the boy, damn it. By the time I talked to him I'd already died a thousand deaths from imagining the worst."

"I'm sorry," Monica said when it registered that Zach's anger was merely his way of expressing his fear.

Zach didn't hear. "Sinclair's out there!" he raged, and gave her a little shake. "Don't you realize how easily he could've grabbed you and Nicky, walking home alone?"

"I'm sorry," Monica said again.

"Yeah." He forced himself to calm down. He raked a hand through his wet hair and looked away. "I thought I'd lost you," he said hoarsely, and his Adam's apple moved as he swallowed.

Monica was overwhelmed by a rush of emotion. She tentatively touched his arm. He looked at it and then at her. "We're fine," she assured him, her own voice a little shaky, too. "Nicky's fine."

"Thank God." Zach's gaze lingered, warmed. "But I wasn't talking about Nicky just now."

"Oh, Zach..." Monica closed her eyes because she didn't dare believe what she thought she'd seen in his. Love? Could it be? Was it possible?

"I'm...so sorry," she said yet again in a ragged whisper.

"Me, too." He cupped her shoulders with his hands and wearily let his forehead come to rest against hers. "It's been hell..."

"For me, too."

"I don't mean just tonight," Zach said.

"I don't, either."

"Monica—" Zach pulled away just far enough to look into her eyes. "For God's sake—"

"Shh." Placing her hands along each side of his face, she tilted her head and, in a move that felt utterly natural and right, sought his mouth with her own.

She felt a spasm of shock tighten Zach's muscles when her lips touched his. And then, with a groan that reverberated almost tangibly upward through his chest, he wrapped his arms around her in a vicelike embrace that squeezed the breath right out of her. And made her a willing prisoner of his almost desperate hunger. A prisoner, and an eager participant.

Everything receded for the duration of their kiss. Fear, anger, all their misunderstandings, every one of Monica's misgivings. They simply ceased to exist. Nothing mattered but this, this fire they kindled between them, this need for each other that seemed to grow stronger each time they kissed.

And when they pulled apart and gazed into each other's eyes, it was with an understanding that, though nothing had visibly changed, neither was everything the same.

"We're going to have to talk about this," Zach said, reluctant to let the interlude end.

Monica nodded, swallowing a lump. "I know."

"Soon."

Biting her lip and averting her brimming eyes, Monica

gave another nod. Not for the life of her could she have spoken just then; too much was coming at her all at once.

As though divining this, Zach gently caught her chin and made her look at him. "We're gonna nail this guy," he vowed. "One way or another. He's not going to hurt you again."

"I know."

"All right then." Zach dropped a light kiss on her lips and stepped away. "Come on, I need to get out of this sopping wet dog suit." He reached past her to open the kitchen door.

But Monica stayed him with just a touch on his arm. "Zach."

"Hmm?"

"Nicole's been awfully quiet. I'm afraid..."

Zach's quick touch to the cheek with the back of his hand told her he understood what she'd left unsaid—that she feared Nicky might have relapsed because of what happened out there on the street. "'S'okay..."

Inside the kitchen, Carla and Pete, carefully pretending not to be curious or concerned about what had gone on in the hall, were unsuccessfully trying to interest Nicole in her Halloween loot.

Monica took a clean kitchen towel out of a drawer. Her eyes indicated Nicky as she handed it to Zach. The little girl had yet to look at either of them. "Here. For your hair."

"Thanks." As Zach obediently toweled his head, he surreptitiously studied Nicky. He didn't like what he saw. The blankness of her expression was frighteningly familiar. Tossing the towel back to Monica, he ran a hand through his hair.

"Hey, squirt..." As he'd often done before, he playfully tugged on one of Nicole's pigtails to get her attention. "Help me with the zipper on this outfit, would you?"

Neither he nor the others could possibly have been prepared for the child's reaction. It was as if by tugging on her hair, Zach had pulled out a plug that had held back a flood of emotions. They burst from her now with a keening wail. She jumped to her feet, tumbling her chair, and ran from the room.

"No," Monica said sharply to her mother and Pete who, their faces ashen with dismay, were up and poised to follow. With a distressed glance at Zach, she hurried after her child.

"Don't worry," Zach reassured the Romanovs as he followed Monica out the door. "We'll handle it..."

Not that he had any idea how. Or whether he would even be welcome. For even though logic told him his gentle tug on Nicole's hair had in no way precipitated her unexpected—and uncharacteristic—outburst, he couldn't help but feel somehow at fault.

He found them by the bathroom that connected to the guest room, the room where Nicky took her naps on those days when they visited.

That is to say, he found Monica. She was rattling the doorknob, slapping the door, begging, cajoling, ordering. "Open up, darling, please. Nicky, let Mommy come in. Open this door, Nicole. Now."

And all the while a stream of silent tears spilled down her anxiety-ravaged face.

From inside could be heard fractured sobs and labored breaths.

"Oh, God, Zach, do something," Monica cried beseechingly when Zach shouldered her aside. "She's locked herself in!"

Zach barely heard her. "Nicole!" He tested the doorknob; it didn't feel very strong. He knew he could easily kick in the door, and fleetingly considered doing just that before dismissing the notion as too dangerous. The bathroom was small. The splintering door could easily injure the child.

"Open the door, Nicky," he said with quiet authority, but without really expecting to be obeyed. In a whispered aside to Monica, he ordered, "Get me a nail. A paper clip, or a piece of wire. Anything that I can use to jimmy the lock."

Monica flew down the stairs to the kitchen while Zach, though feeling anything but calm, talked to the child in a calm, soothing voice. Her very quietness terrified him.

"You know we love you, Nicky," he said. "Your mommy and I. And Grandma and Pete, Ada and Mitch. None of us would let anybody hurt you, sweetheart. I promise. But don't touch anything in the cabinets you know you shouldn't. All right, sweetheart? Honey, Charlie needs you to come home."

The door opened. Zach took one look at the sorry sight that was Nicole and dropped to his knees. "Oh, baby." He gathered her into his arms. "Sweetheart, what've you done?"

He held her tight, rocking her small form, crooning, while she burrowed into him with little whimpers that tore at his heart so that he had to close his eyes to contain the pressure of tears he had not shed since Maddy's tragic death. "Oh, baby, baby..."

From behind him, a gasp. And then Monica, on the floor next to him, eyes widened with horrified disbelief.

She would have cried out, but Zach sharply shook his head, unmindful of the tears that wouldn't be stemmed when he opened his eyes to focus them quellingly on Monica.

She slumped, burying her face in her hands.

Another noise drew Zach's attention. Carla and Pete, silent, concerned, had come into the room. Carla's eyes went from Zach's to the small form nestled against him. And what she saw made a hand fly to her mouth. Blindly, she turned into Pete's embrace.

Zach locked eyes with the man. He mouthed, "Doc Koontz," and was relieved when Pete indicated his comprehension with a curt nod.

He bent to his wife, whispered something, and gently

pressed her down on a nearby chair. Moments later, Zach could hear the gravelly murmur of Pete's voice on the master bedroom phone.

He stiffened when Nicole stirred in his arms. He loosened his hold, allowed her head to come up. They looked at each other.

Next to him he felt more than saw Monica raise her head.

He kept his focus on Nicole. Her large brown eyes were rimmed in red, her silky lashes a tangle of spikes. Her face was tear-stained and flushed.

And above it was the ruin of her hacked-off hair.

Zach couldn't speak. He only hoped that all the love he felt for this child was there in his eyes for her to see.

"Oh, Nicky..." It was Monica, her voice a breathy whisper, but full of love and now remarkably steady. Until an errant sob broke from her throat and undid her. "Why?"

Nicole disengaged herself from Zach and put her arms around Monica's neck. "Don't...cry...M-M-Mommy," she said haltingly in a voice that was scratchy and hoarse.

And to which everyone in the room listened with amazement.

"Don't...want...to...look..." She struggled with the words, shaping soundless ones to every one that could be heard. Her breathing grew agitated, frustration darkened her eyes.

But when Monica tried to calm her with a soothing, "I know, love, I know," she vehemently shook her head.

Her little hands clenched into fists and she stamped her foot in the first show of unbridled temper any of them had ever seen her display. And the words burst out in a torrent. "Don't want to look like Nicky no more. Daddy's here. Daddy's here..."

Over and over, the same words. Louder and louder. Punctuated by the fists she pounded on the floor after collapsing there in an out-of-control heap.

And it was on Zach that she pounded when he finally managed to confine her writhing form in his arms. He held her, letting her punches land where they may and letting her rage, if that was what is was, run its course.

He didn't know how long it took; long enough, it seemed, for the doctor to come to the house. Nicky had subsided into whimpering sobs by then and didn't protest when Monica took her from Zach.

Nor did she struggle when, at the doctor's silent direction, Monica laid her on the bed. Her hand spasmed briefly in Monica's when the doctor injected her with a mild sedative.

"Nothing to worry about," he assured Monica. "It'll just let her sleep soundly till the morning, without disturbing dreams."

Monica found them all around the kitchen table when she finally came down. Carla had heated up and served some soup, she noted. And the men had apparently made short shrift of it, judging by the empty bowls in front of them.

Looking down at the swath of silky red tresses in her hands through the distortion of her tears, she doubted she'd be able to swallow even a bite of food any time soon.

"She's asleep," she said to no one in particular.

"Poor mite," Carla said, pressing a wadded tissue to the corner of her eyes. "Poor darling little mite..."

"She spoke," Doc Koontz said with matter-of-fact gruffness. "Let's not lose sight of that amid all this moaning and bewailing."

He turned to Zach. "I told you it might take something traumatic." He sternly included everyone else once again. "And you can't expect her to come out from behind years of self-containment and silence with a polite little howdy-do. She'll be fine. She's a kid, they're resilient. And the last thing she needs from any of you now is to be treated like a seventh wonder or, just as bad, a recovering invalid.

"Don't be expecting her to talk up a storm now, either.

I doubt she'll say much at all for the next little while. A word here and there. Maybe. Or maybe more. We'll just have to see. Needless to say, what she doesn't need now is any more trauma.''

He got up. "I got other calls to make. Babies to deliver." He grabbed up his bag. "I'll see myself out. Call me in the morning if you need to."

"Want some soup, dear?" Carla asked, breaking the dazed silence that had hung over the room in the wake of the doctor's departure. They were all exhausted. Zach, finally out of the Dalmatian costume, sported a purpling bruise where one of Nicole's punches had connected with his cheek bone.

"No, thanks." Monica found a Ziploc bag in one of the drawers and stuffed the hair inside.

"Throw that away," her mother urged softly.

"No." Monica shook her head, her voice sharp. She gentled it. "No, Ma. I can't."

She looked at Zach. "It *was* Richard out there, that much we can now be sure of. Nicky recognized his voice. He terrified her. We can't let him get to her."

"The only way he will," Zach vowed grimly, "is over my dead body."

"Don't even think something like that." Monica hugged herself against the sudden chill raising goose bumps on her skin. "You don't know what he's capable of."

"Oh, I think I have a pretty good idea." Zach's lip curled with contempt. "He's a real tough guy with women and children. But he runs pretty fast when there's men around."

"Couldn't catch him, eh?" Pete said. It was one of those innocuous statements of the obvious that people tended to make when saddled with a feeling of helplessness.

"Nah." Zach was much too inherently courteous to offer less than a proper reply. "People everywhere. And he wore a black jacket. It's a cinch he took off that mask. He just sort of vanished into the crowd. But I needed to try..."

"Sure you did," Pete said.

Zach looked at Monica. She was at the sink, getting a drink of water. "I need a picture of him," Zach told her because it just occurred to him that he had no idea what the man looked like, except from the back. "Give me a picture I can make color copies from and pass out around town and to the men at Windemeer."

"A picture?" Monica repeated incredulously. "You don't seriously expect me to carry pictures of that man around with me, do you?"

Zach grimaced. "I guess not. How about in your things? Any photo albums?"

"No, nothing," Monica said unhappily. "After the divorce and everything, I took out all of Nicky's pictures and burned the rest." She met Zach's gaze. "I wish now I hadn't."

But he was glad she had. It demonstrated the finality with which she'd severed her bonds to Sinclair, and that was important to him.

He gave her a weary smile. "It was just a thought."

"I think I might still have a picture around here somewhere," Carla suddenly said. She got up. "Let me just look in that box I keep in the hall closet."

While Monica began to clear the table and Zach got up to help her, Carla bustled out. Pete, with a muttered excuse, departed through the back door.

"He's gone to sneak a smoke," Monica whispered to Zach, and they shared a halfhearted smile that vanished as quickly as it had come.

Monica set up the drain board. "What a night," she said on a shivery sigh. "I'll have to have her hair cut properly tomorrow."

"Couldn't you do it yourself?" Zach asked, taking a tea towel off the rack as Monica began to wash the dishes.

"I'm not sure taking her to a salon would be such a good idea. Sinclair's out there."

"You're right. Of course, you're right." Monica bit her lip, sorrowfully shaking her head. "Her beautiful hair..."

"Will grow back," Zach said with some of Doc's earlier asperity. "Look, Monica, you've got to let go of it. It's not the end of the world. Let's concentrate on the positive. She talked. Think of what a breakthrough that is."

"You're right. I'm sorry." She tried to push a strand of hair out of her face with the back of her soapy hand. It promptly slid back down. "I'm just tired."

"It's been one hell of a day," Zach said, taking hold of her chin and turning her face toward him so he could secure the errant lock. "You're entitled to be tired."

He would probably have given in to the urge to kiss her if Carla hadn't chosen that moment to return to the kitchen.

"I found one," she said. "Your wedding picture," she said to Monica, extending a glossy five-by-seven with an almost apologetic glance at Zach.

While Monica dried her hands, Zach took the picture. His glance at Sinclair was cursory. Just long enough to establish that ten years ago the man still had a full head of hair and eyes that were set too close together.

The woman in virgin white bridal regalia merited closer scrutiny. She was lovely. And she was gazing at her groom in a way an inner voice told him she would never look at him.

He raised his eyes and they almost audibly clashed with Monica's. She was shaken by what she saw—pain, and something else.

Quietly she said, "I was very young."

"And very much in love," Zach said, the mildness of this observation masking an emotion that was like some ugly viper writhing in his gut. Jealousy. He had never experienced it before, and he didn't like it one bit.

Nor did he like what it prompted him to do, which was to rip the picture in two, right down the middle. "I won't be needing that," he clipped, and let the part that depicted the bride carelessly drop to the floor. "Will I?"

Ignoring the inner voice that said, *You're acting like a jerk,* he snatched his denim jacket off the back of his chair and, with just the barest of nods and a muttered good-night to Carla, slammed out the back door.

Monica could hear Pete hail him there, but Zach's reply, if he made one, was indistinct.

Moments later Pete came into the kitchen. "That Zach sure was in an all-fired hurry all of a sudden." His eyes went from Carla, who was looking at her daughter with concerned bewilderment, to Monica, still reeling from Zach's uncharacteristic behavior. "Something happen here I should know about?"

Monica helplessly shook her head. Leaving her mother to explain or not, she bent to pick up the discarded scrap of photograph and quickly walked to the door. "I'm really very tired," she said in a strangled voice. "I think I'll just…"

Her eyes met her mother's and the look of commiseration there made it impossible to say more. With another quick shake of the head, she turned and fled the room.

Up in the guest room, she didn't turn on the light for fear of disturbing Nicole who slumbered in the twin bed on the other side of the nightstand. After checking on her child and dropping a featherlight kiss on the now serenely smoothed forehead, she undressed in the bathroom and slipped into the long flannel nightgown her mother had thoughtfully put out for her, along with an unused toothbrush. She washed her face, brushed her teeth and rinsed out her briefs, moving like an automaton, barely aware of what she was doing.

And all the while she stared at the picture of herself that she had tucked into the mirror's frame and tried to discover what had caused Zach the kind of pain she had seen in his eyes.

Pain, and something else. Some *thing,* some *emotion*

that had turned them glittery and hard. Anger? No. She had seen him angry; his eyes were like a stormy sky at those times.

Jealousy? *Pshaw*. Monica felt silly even thinking the word in connection with Zach. And yet...

I was very young, she had told him. And she had been. Less so in years—she'd been twenty-three, after all—as in terms of worldliness and sophistication. She'd been gullible, naive, and incredibly flattered to have someone as confident and suave as Richard Sinclair single her out. Eight years older, eons wiser in the ways of men and women, he had been, to her, a charmer.

She'd been a virgin, a product of parochial schools, and the sheltered only child of Carla and Thomas Griffith. Premarital sex was a no-no.

And Richard, used to easy conquests, had been intrigued enough by Monica's virginal shyness and reticence to outdo himself in his pursuit of her. A whirlwind courtship culminated in a storybook wedding.

Romantic novels always ended with the wedding night. And so did Monica's romance with Richard Sinclair, right along with her dreams of happily-ever-after.

The very inexperience and shyness that had so tantalized Richard before the nuptials were a crashing bore to him afterward. He took her virginity with painful roughness that satiny, flower-scented night in their Honolulu hotel. But for the rest of their fourteen-day honeymoon in the Islands, and beyond, he usually sought his pleasures elsewhere.

But, of course, the starry-eyed girl in the photograph had had no inkling of what lay in store for her. She had been so very young...

And so very much in love, Zach had countered when she'd said that to him. And she had been—in love with love. The idea of it, the girlish dream of it. None of which had anything at all to do with the woman she was today.

Or, more to the point, with the kind of love she had come to feel for Zacharius Robinson.

Zach had awakened in her a yearning for completeness. A need to give, to share, to have, to hold. To give him children, happiness. To be in all things his...mate.

Yet Zach didn't know this. She had never told him. Not with words—she'd been too afraid. And apparently not with her eyes, either. Which, she supposed, shouldn't really come as a surprise to her, since the woman she'd become had long since learned that it was dangerous to wear her heart on her sleeve.

Now, though, she felt strong enough to change all that. First chance. As to the bride in that picture...

Monica tugged the photo away from the mirror and ripped it to shreds. She raised the toilet lid, dropped in the pieces and flushed. "Good riddance," she whispered. And went to bed.

She was roused from a restless sleep as the dawn just barely began to brighten the undraped glass of the guest room window. Uncertain as to what had caused her to wake, Monica raised up on one elbow and peered intently over at Nicole. The night-light that was plugged into an outlet on the wall shed just enough light to allow her to make out her child's features. They were relaxed in slumber, and she was breathing deeply and regularly through her slightly open mouth.

No bangs obscured the purity of her high forehead. Instead, a ragged fringe served as a painful reminder of everything that had happened the previous night.

There. Monica froze in a listening attitude. A ping against the window. And another.

Sure now that this was what had awakened her, Monica tossed back the covers and got out of bed. She tiptoed to the window. Peered out into the murky semidarkness. Reflexively jerked back as another pebble struck the glass, making any remnants of sleepiness vanish.

Who in the world? She cautiously brought her face close to the glass again, holding her breath so as not to fog it up. She cupped her hands on each side of her eyes and at first could make out only the asphalt tiles of the front porch roof just below. A movement drew her attention beyond the roof and downward. And then she saw him. Wearing the same ball cap, jeans and fleece-lined denim jacket as last night, with the collar turned up against the damp chill of early morning, he was standing just inside the gate of her mother's front yard. Behind him, his Suburban was parked at the curb.

Zach. He had spotted her, too, now and was beckoning her to come down.

It never occurred to Monica not to go to him. She hurried into the bathroom as soundlessly as a ghost. She rinsed her mouth, ran a brush through her hair and quickly got into her clothes. Her ankle boots were downstairs in the hall closet with her coat. She tiptoed down the stairs in her stocking feet, cringing and holding her breath as first one step creaked and then another.

The front door hinges, too, could use a squirt of oil, she thought with a grimace as she eased it open after slipping into her boots and coat. She hurried across the porch and down the shallow steps at the bottom of which Zach stood waiting.

"How's Nicky?" he asked in a worried half whisper.

"Asleep." Monica stopped one step up from the bottom, which left her at eye level with him. She studied his face, wondered if it was the murky light of dawn or fatigue that was making his skin look gray. Had his concern for Nicole kept him up all night? Or was the fault with her?

"What're you doing here?" she asked, shivering as a gust of moisture-laden wind swept around the corner of the house and whipped open her coat. She wrapped it around herself and folded her arms to hold it in place. "Has something happened? Is something wrong?"

"Yes," Zach said, "to both of those questions. Nothing

to do with Nicole," he reassured her quickly, clasping her around the shoulders and pulling her with him through the gate toward his truck. "And I haven't made copies of the picture yet. Everything's closed."

"Well, no wonder—it's the dead of night."

"I've been driving around—"

"Oh, Zach."

"Calling myself twelve kinds of a fool." He opened the door and hustled her inside. "Don't worry," he said. "I'm not abducting you. It's warmer and more private in there, that's all."

He closed the door behind her and walked around to the driver's side.

"I never thought you were planning to abduct me," Monica said as Zach settled himself behind the wheel. "And you're not a fool."

"Then maybe you show more faith in me than I deserve."

"I don't think so."

They looked at each other in silence for a moment. And then they both spoke at once.

"About tonight, I—"

"Zach, about that picture—"

They stopped, again as if on cue. Monica bit her lip to hold back a nervous giggle.

Zach, angled toward her with his left arm draped over the steering wheel, pressed his mouth against the knuckles of that hand with a rueful little chuckle. "Guess I'll go first," he said, gazing out at the empty street through the windshield for a moment before resolutely swinging his eyes back to Monica's.

"Rebecca would tell you, if you asked, that I *hate* to apologize—"

"Then don't," Monica interrupted, impulsively putting a hand over his right one, resting on his thigh. She immediately pulled it away again when Zach's eyes homed in on it.

"You've done nothing to apologize for," she finished, a little self-consciously because, in retrospect, the quick withdrawal of her hand struck her as foolish. Something that girl in the picture might have done, but not the woman of poise and maturity she had told herself she'd become.

"I was incredibly rude to storm off the way I did," Zach said, making no comment about the touch of Monica's hand, or giving any indication of the fact that he very much wanted her to feel free to touch him anywhere, anytime. "It was that picture," he admitted gruffly. "On top of everything else you and I've been going 'round and 'round about..."

"You mean, the...marriage thing?" Monica said when Zach seemed to flounder.

"Yeah." He stared up at the sky where a new day was dawning. "The way you looked at him..."

"Represents just one moment in time," Monica exclaimed. "And the image has very little to do with reality. You were married yourself once, for heaven's sake. And I'm sure there were pictures taken on your wedding day, too. Pictures that show you smiling and happy and full of optimism about the future. Am I right?"

"I guess you are," Zach said. Ruefully.

"Well then, with everything that's happened between that day and now, would you say those two people in the photograph are who you and your ex-wife are today?"

"Lord, no." Zach choked on a bitter little laugh, but his eyes were very serious when he added, "What you're saying not only makes sense, it makes me feel like an even bigger idiot than before. I'm sorry. All I can say in my defense is..."

Lord, but this was hard, he thought, first thing in the morning and on an empty stomach. He took a deep breath. "I was jealous. For the simple—or not so simple—reason that I—I've been wanting you...to look at me...the way you looked at him. There. I've said it."

He glared at her, his expression one of embarrassed defiance.

Monica, whose mind was reeling from the implications of Zach's admission, thought he looked like a grumpy little boy "fessing up." It made her want to hug him and say, "It's all right."

"Oh, Zach." She caught his hand in both of hers. "Don't you see? There's no way I could possibly ever look at you like that because, for better or worse, I'm simply not—" *That person anymore,* she meant to tell him before reiterating the conclusions she had drawn in the bathroom last night. But Zach wouldn't let her finish.

"I know that," he interrupted with quiet emphasis. Withdrawing his hand, he did his damnedest not to let his disappointment show. After all, he had known that what she felt for him, what he was able to *make* her feel with his kisses was, at best, nothing more than passion coupled with a certain grateful fondness.

"And that's what I came to tell you," he said. "That I don't expect you to be in love with me. Even if you do decide to marry me, it's okay.

"Don't." He put a finger across Monica's lips when she wanted to speak, to tell him he was wrong, that he understood nothing, that he had it all backward. "Don't say anything more. Just know that no matter what, I'm your friend. Yours and Nicole's. The rest can wait."

"But, Zach..." Monica removed his silencing finger with more than a hint of impatience. "You don't understand..."

"I do." He leaned forward and dropped a light kiss on her lips, then swiveled away and, to Monica's utter frustration, concluded the discussion by getting out of the truck.

She was out of her side before he'd rounded the hood to offer assistance. "So help me, Zach Robinson, you are the most aggravating individual I've ever had the misfortune to try to have a conversation with. Listen to me, darn you.''

She scrambled after him when he simply turned on his heel and began walking toward the house. She grabbed him by the arm, and when that didn't make him stop, squeezed alongside of him through the garden gate before blocking his path with her body. ''I'm trying to tell you something!''

''And I'm sure the neighbors are just dying to hear what that is,'' her mother's voice said from above them on the porch. Her hair wound up in rollers, she was wearing her heavy chenille robe over her nightgown, the newspaper she'd come out to collect clutched in her hand.

She was eyeing Monica and Zach with a decidedly appalled expression. ''What in the world are you two carrying on about at a time like this, and at such an ungodly hour?''

Monica knew when she was licked. Besides, she decided, Zach was right, even if it was for all the wrong reasons. This was not the time for her to declare her feelings for him. Or, indeed, to make plans for the future. First things first. And those first things were the same as they'd been all along—Nicole's safety and well-being.

''I suppose I could let Roger handle this by himself,'' Zach said a couple of days later, unhappy and undecided about leaving Windemeer. He was convinced that Sinclair was on the island and, no doubt, just waiting to make his move.

''Don't be ridiculous.'' Monica knew how important it was for Zach to go. It wasn't just airplane parts they were after on this trip to Seattle, it was a whole new aircraft. A second float plane, which would greatly enhance the scope of their charter operation. And which Zach had waited a long time to be able to afford.

Well, one had come on the market—used, but apparently in mint condition. There was no way Roger Creswell could fly down to the lower forty-eight and make the purchasing decision on his own.

"We'll be fine," Monica assured Zach, determined not to be a hindrance to him in the conduct of his business by letting her anxieties show. "Mitch and Deke'll still be here.

"And don't forget Ada," she added in an attempt to joke, nodding her head toward the old housekeeper who was stoically peeling potatoes behind them at the sink.

Zach responded as Monica had hoped. He grinned, and quipped loud enough for Ada to hear, "You're right. Just looking into that sour puss of hers would scare anybody off."

"Guess some of us in this kitchen don't want no supper tonight, is what I'm thinkin'," Ada said to no one in particular, though she winked at Nicole who stood on a footstool next to her, haphazardly scraping carrots.

"Stew," Nicole announced in that peculiarly scratchy voice of hers that never failed to arrest Monica's attention. And Zach's.

"Stew, huh?" Zach half turned his head with a smile of approval. "Wouldn't want to miss that so I guess I'd better behave."

Monica chuckled, swiveling in her chair to fully face her daughter. Her eyes swept past the kitchen's side window as she twisted her torso around. She froze.

"Zach..." She groped for his hand. "He's out there."

Chapter Ten

Zach asked no questions. He was out of his chair and out of the kitchen, whistling for Zeus, before Ada had even turned from the sink to ask, "What's the matter?"

If she hadn't been so paralyzed with reaction, Monica might have marveled at the speed with which a man of Zach's age and size could move. It took her a lot longer to get to her feet and when she finally stood, her knees knocked so hard she was bound to sport bruises there tomorrow.

It was clear to her that she would be of no help to Zach outside at all. She barely made it over to the sink to hover protectively near her child who, blessedly oblivious, continued to hack at her carrots with total concentration.

"I thought I saw someone," Monica said quietly in reply to Ada's question. She knew she didn't have to spell out who. She pressed a hand to her head, shaking it. "Some hero I am, when the chips are down."

"Well, now, girl," Ada said, wiping her hands on her apron before gently guiding Monica back to a chair, "don't be too hard on yourself. We none of us know what we can or can't do until the time comes to find out."

She turned her head to the door as Zach strode back into the room. "Anything?"

"Nope."

He went over to Monica, who slumped in her chair. "Now I feel like a fool," she told him with profound self-disgust. "Worse than that, a cowardly fool."

"Don't be silly." Zach hunkered down in front of her and took her hands. They were cold as ice. He chafed them between both of his and kept his voice low. "Deke saw a car parked out back behind the hangar a while ago. It's gone now."

"But..." Monica frowned. "Could you-know-who have gotten back there so quickly, and without being seen?" She withdrew her hands, tucked them into her armpits and hunched her shoulders. Her nerves were wound too tightly already, even without Zach's disturbing touch. "And wouldn't Deke have seen or heard him drive away?"

"Unlikely." Zach got to his feet. "When I got there, Deke was testing the engine on the one-eighty-two after giving it a tune-up. A herd of elephants could've run by without him hearing a thing. I told him no more engine testing. What good're alarms and safety measures if they can't be heard or attended to?"

"Or maybe I was simply seeing things." Monica jumped to her feet. "I've got to do something constructive or go crazy. Ada, will you let me bake a cake?"

Refusal was written all over the older woman's face. "Well, now..." she started to say.

But said no more when Nicky clapped her hands and cried, "Yes. Cake..." She dragged her footstool to the cupboard and got out the canister of flour. "Mommy. I help you..."

With a disgruntled glance at Zach that seemed to say, *See what I've gotta put up with?* Ada shuffled back to the sink. "Just don't you leave me no messes to clean up," she huffed. "'Cause I ain't gonna do it. No sir."

By noon the next day, Zach and Roger were en route to Seattle. Zach and Monica had gone 'round and 'round about it both the night before and this morning, with Zach saying he'd stay and Monica, chagrined about her performance of the previous day, insisting he go.

But even so, Zach had called one more meeting of the Windemeer residents and crew that morning and gone over the precautions and instructions he'd issued, and which everyone knew by heart.

The only place Monica and Nicole were allowed to be was either in the house or in the office. They could walk around outside only if accompanied by Mitch or Deke.

Ada was not considered an adequate guardian, a decree which she heartily and vociferously resented.

Only the Romanovs and Doc Koontz were approved visitors, but under no circumstances were Monica and Nicky to go into town. Not even with the Romanovs.

"I'm only going to be gone three days max," Zach said in a tone that brooked no dissension as he, accompanied by Monica and Nicole, strode over to where the Cessna and Roger Creswell stood ready for takeoff. "Surely that's not long enough for you to get cabin fever."

He squatted in front of Nicky. "I hear you have a birthday coming up, Punkin face. What would you like me to bring you for a present? A new dress?"

"Nuh-uh." Nicole shook her head. With her hair cropped close to the scalp à la Joan of Arc, she was an adorable little pixie. "I wanna...b—bi..." She screwed up her face and finally got the word out. "A...*bikesissle!*"

"Ah." Zach's brows arched. "And do you know how to ride one of those?"

Nicole again shook her head, an expression of worried uncertainty gathering on her face.

With a furtive wink at Monica, Zach mused, "I suppose she *could* learn."

"Oh, I'm sure she could." Though she increasingly felt like bursting into tears, Monica mustered a shaky smile. With all her heart she wished Zach would stay, even though she, herself, had kept urging him to go. She would miss him, would have missed him even without the threat of Sinclair's presence. She wished there was some way she could tell Zach just what he'd come to mean to her. But the time for tender confessions still wasn't right. Sometimes she despaired that it ever would be.

How good he was to them, to Nicole. He doted on the child but without being overindulgent. And he always seemed to know just how to talk to her, interact with her.

Like now, narrowing his eyes and puckering his forehead as he asked Nicole, "So, how old're you gonna be? Sixteen?"

"No." Nicole giggled. "Six, you silly."

"Ah..." Grinning back, Zach ruffled her hair and straightened. "As it happens, six is just about the right age to be getting a bike."

With a squeal of delight, Nicole launched herself at him and he spun her around as expected. The moment her feet were back on the ground, she sped off to spread the news.

Zach turned to Monica. "Have Pete pick her up a bike in town and hide it in the hangar where I can find it when I get back."

"All right." Monica's voice was a little scratchy. Alone with him now, her emotions threatened to get the best of her, after all.

"Th-thank you," she stammered, suddenly shy beneath his silent, and now somber, regard. "Nicky—"

"Forget Nicky," Zach said brusquely. It killed him to leave. "What about you?"

Monica blinked. "M-me?"

"Anything *you* want from Seattle?"

"No. There's nothing." Gazing up at him, all the love

she felt for him clamored for expression. To heck with the timing, she thought, and told him what was in her heart, "Because everything any woman could ever want is…right here.

"Any woman?" Zach asked after a long and profound silence during which he searched her eyes with unsettling intensity. He took her hand and brought it to his lips. "Even…this one?"

"Especially this one," Monica whispered.

And melted into him when Zach pulled her into his arms for a hot and thorough kiss.

"Hold that thought," he told her with another hard kiss. And before climbing into the pilot seat, added, "And after I'm back we're finally gonna get things settled."

Monica could only nod, not that he would have heard her reply over the noise of the Cessna's engine. Emotion had once again choked her up, but she lifted her hand in a farewell salute and held his gaze as long as she could. *I'll be here, Zach.*

But as she watched until the plane was nothing more than a speck in the sky, she hugged herself against a sudden chill and wished she had said the words out loud.

After lunch in the kitchen with Ada, Monica went to the office to catch up on some of the paperwork she'd gotten behind on while working on those Halloween costumes.

Nicole had gone with Mitch to the barn, where he had stuff to do, and Nicky played with Charlie as well as Zelda's two remaining pups that hadn't yet been sold. Nicole loved to boss her roly-poly little charges around, making them sit and stay and come with varying degrees of success and a whole lot of high-pitched giggling and yipping.

Monica was on the floor in front of one of the file cabinets, immersed in a book she had chanced across in its bottom drawer. A scrapbook, she'd discovered. Full of yel-

lowed clippings and photographs both amateur and professional, all of which were about Zacharius Robinson, the
basketball star.

She had the radio tuned to an Oldies station and was
listening with half an ear to a mellow rendition of "Canadian Sunset." The rest of her concentration was focused
on the young woman whose extraordinary beauty even a
grainy newspaper photograph had not been able to distort.
She was dressed in an elegant suit and next to her with his
arm around her waist, also in a suit, looking young and—
so Monica thought—kind of sappy, was Zach.

The caption above the picture read: Bad Boy Of Basketball Bags Beauty Queen.

Monica rolled her eyes. *Talk about corny...*

Of course it could just be possible that she was simply
jealous. Until she reminded herself that not only had Zach
divorced this former beauty queen, the woman had in the
meantime grown some twenty years older.

"I'll bet she's a matronly frump by now," Monica muttered, and flipped the page with a chuckle at her own foolishness.

She heard the office door open and close and quickly
replaced the book in the drawer. She was supposed to be
working, for heaven's sake.

"Is that you, Deke?" she called as a heavy tread that
was unmistakably male could be heard moving toward her
from the door. "I'm down here," she said a little breath-
lessly as she scrambled to her feet.

She turned with a smile. "I was just—" The words
froze in her throat.

"Hello, Monica," Richard Sinclair said. He sauntered
toward her, glancing around. "Not much of an office for
the lucrative charter business your boyfriend's reputed to
have going here for himself."

It was so stupid, Monica knew it even as the words came
out of her mouth. But all she could think of to say as she

watched the man of her nightmares approach her with unmistakably evil intent, was, "Zach is not my boyfriend."

"No?" Sinclair said, disinterested. He shrugged. "Whatever." And stopped at Monica's desk to flip through the letters she had typed on the computer and just printed out.

"I see that year in secretarial school I put you through has paid off."

"The only thing you ever put me through was hell," Monica said coldly.

She had no idea how or when, and wasn't about to question her good fortune, but all traces of fear had vanished. In its stead she felt an icy calm, coupled with an iron determination that, no matter what, she would not let him get anywhere near Nicole.

She stared at him with frigid contempt when, with an unpleasant smile, he drawled, "My, my, haven't we gotten feisty."

He stepped up to her, so close she could smell his aftershave. It was the same he'd always used—expensive, discreet. It made her gag.

She stiffened when he chucked her beneath the chin. "Maybe it's been too long since I taught you respect," he said. And in a move so quick that Monica could neither brace herself nor see it coming, he backhanded her across the face.

Her head snapped sideways and back. An involuntary gasp escaped her. She immediately compressed her lips, remembering only too well how much pleasure this man derived out of hearing her cry out.

She put all the hatred she felt for him into the glare she fixed on his face. "Don't you ever strike me again."

She dodged past him before he could react and stop her. She ran to her phone. The letter H. That's all she had to punch to activate an alarm.

Sinclair's hand slammed down on top of hers. With his other hand he grabbed her hair and yanked back her head as he pulled her away from the desk. "We've got business, you and I," he snarled. "Where's the kid?"

"As if I would tell you," Monica raged, twisting her torso this way and that until she was turned toward him enough to knee him in the groin.

Doubling over, clutching himself, he released her. She gave him a hard shove that knocked him off balance and sprinted for the door. Just short of it, he tackled her. They crashed to the floor. Monica's face connected with it, hard. She saw stars. Blinked back blackness. Tasted blood.

Her head was yanked back again. He had her once more by the hair. Something sticky and warm was dripping into her eyes, blinding her. She clawed at his hands.

"Where's the kid?"

He got to his feet, dragging her up with him. Still by the hair. Shaking her. She dug the nails of both hands into his arms as hard as she could. With an oath, he let go. She spun. Faced him. Kicked out at him. Clawed at him...

Voices. High-pitched. "Mommy! Daddy! Noo-oo!"

Nicky! Not sure if she yelled it. Meant to. *Nicky, run!*

Another scream. *Nicky!*

A savage growl, a bark. A crash. The furious snarl of a dog. Zeus. A curse and a howl of pain. High-pitched and frantic puppy yipping...

The dogs. Thank God.

Monica wiped at the blood in her eyes to clear her vision, to find her child. And finally spotted her cowering beneath Zach's desk, pale as a ghost, eyes wide with terror, both fists pressed to her mouth. In front of her, yips interspersed with fierce puppy growls, Charlie stood guard.

"Nicky...." Monica sank to her knees, crawled to her child, gathered her up and held on tight. "Oh, baby...."

Just then Mitch burst into the room with Deke only moments behind. They looked around wildly, briefly zeroed in on her and Nicole and, seeing them relatively safe, turned their attention to the side. Monica's eyes followed them.

And that's when she saw him—Richard Sinclair, flat on his back with one hundred and fifty pounds of growling and panting malamute standing over him, poised to attack if he moved as much as an eyelash.

"Zeus!" Mitch ordered. "Release!"

The huge dog obeyed, but slowly and with obvious reluctance. The timbre of his growl increased as he backed away. His piercing blue eyes with their pinpricks of black pupil did not release the man from their menacing stare.

Without ceremony, Mitch and Deke hauled Richard Sinclair to his feet. It was just as well they had no intention of letting go of him, because he swayed like a drunk and his knees kept buckling. His fancy leather jacket sported several large rips, and one of the sleeves was torn down past his elbow, exposing a bleeding gash that was most certainly courtesy of Zeus.

"I called the police and the Doc." It was Ada, rushing into the room. She spat on the floor as she walked past Sinclair, but homed instantly in on Monica and Nicole.

"Out!" she ordered. No hand-wringing and tut-tutting for her. "Come, come, come." She bent as if to drag them out from beneath the desk, but the touch of her hands was surprisingly gentle.

Or maybe not so surprisingly, since both Nicky and Monica knew by now what Zach had know for years, namely that Ada was a fraud. That beneath all the bluster and crankiness beat a heart as soft as slush and as big as the state that was her native land.

By the time Doc Koontz arrived, Ada had mother and daughter cleaned up and tucked into bed with hot water bottles and plenty of scolding.

"That nose o' yours is broke, my girl," she said to Monica in a tone that clearly indicated that this had been done just to irk her. "You see if the Doc don't agree."

He did, of course, cheerfully adding that it looked like Monica would have two black eyes to add to the overall effect. "Too bad Halloween's over. You could'a gone as a raccoon."

If she hadn't already been so groggy from the sedative he'd administered, Monica would gladly have repaid Doc's warped sense of humor by blackening one of his eyes in return.

As it was, she hugged to herself his assurance that Nicole had not lapsed back into silence, and that aside from a good dose of terror, she had not been physically harmed.

The last thing she saw before she lapsed into drug-induced sleep, was her mother's face, careworn and pale. "Don't worry, Ma," she murmured. "Everything's... okay...."

When she awakened, Zach sat by her bed. Though she didn't know it, he had been there for more than twelve hours now, ever since he'd gotten home, late the previous night.

The trip to Seattle had been a bust. The float plane had already been sold. Roger had opted to stay for a few days of vacation, but Zach had turned right around and caught the next commercial flight back to Anchorage. On edge, partly from anticipation of finally getting things settled between Monica and himself, but also from a peculiar sense of fear, he had flown the Cessna straight home from there.

He hadn't slept since his return to Windemeer. Couldn't. Didn't want to. Because being awake, looking into the ruins of Monica's face, helped to remind him that he was to blame for those cuts and the bruises, both physical and mental. He had promised her safety, assured her of his personal protection.

He'll only get to you over my dead body, he had arrogantly boasted to her only a few short days before. And yet it was *her* body that had ended up very nearly dead.

He had failed. For the second time in his life he had failed to be there, failed to live up to his obligations by failing to keep safe the ones he loved.

It didn't matter that this time no one had died. Nor did it matter that the culprit—Sinclair—was behind bars, and that he, Zach, would do everything in his power to see that the man never came near Monica and Nicole again.

He had failed. And knowing that was even harder to bear than the terrible certainty that, once recovered, Monica was bound to be leaving.

After all, he'd failed to keep his spoken promise to her—*I'll keep you safe.* He could hardly expect her to keep an *uns*poken promise to him, one he'd read in her eyes, but most likely had only imagined, *I'll be there.*

"Zach?"

The hesitant whisper of his name abruptly yanked Zach from his dark reverie. He bent over Monica, forcing a smile. "How do you feel?"

"How do I look?" Monica countered feebly, drowsy in spite of the surge of joy that she'd felt at the sight of him.

"Beautiful," Zach said hoarsely, and traced a finger along the curve of her cheek and jaw with such tenderness that an ache of emotion in the throat added itself to all the other pains and discomforts Monica suffered already.

"Liar."

"All right then, terrible."

"Well, you should see the other guy," she quipped weakly, reaching up to catch hold of Zach's hand, trapping it next to her cheek.

Zach said grimly, "I already did." Catching the look of concern in her eyes, he hastened to gentle his tone. "But all that can wait till later. For now, let's just be glad that it's done. Hmm?"

Monica searched his eyes. He seemed to be acting so strangely. "Is it...done?"

"Oh, yes." There was that grimness again.

It scared her somehow. "Are *you* all right?" She held on to his hand when he would have pulled it away. "Zach?"

"I'm fine." Zach forced himself to look at her. To smile. "A little tired, that's all."

"I know what you mean." Monica yawned and her eyelids fluttered. But she didn't let go of his hand. "Stay awhile. My head hurts...."

"I'm sorry," Zach murmured. "So sorry..."

It's not your fault, Monica wanted to assure him, but sleep claimed her before the words could come out.

The next time she woke, Ada was there, greeting her with a disgruntled, "Well, it's about time."

Monica smiled as best she could. "I'm glad to see you, too."

"How you feelin'?" Ada fussed with the blankets.

"Better, I think." Unperturbed by Ada's gruffness, Monica carefully shifted her gaze. The room didn't spin around her this time and her head no longer felt as if it was going to splinter into pieces. "Where's Zach?"

"Minding that daughter o' yours. She's been a handful..."

Nicky.

"Oh, my God, Ada..." Monica surged up from the pillow, only to sink back with a gasp as a stab of pain lacerated her skull. She closed her eyes and pressed a hand to her pounding forehead. "Is...she...all right?"

"I reckon she will be as soon's she can see you."

"Oh, please..."

"Okay, okay." Her gentle hands belying the ferocity of her expression, Ada smoothed some hair out of Monica's face. "Just for a minute now, hear?"

Zach firmly kept hold of Nicole's little hand as he led the child into the room. He didn't want her rushing in and flinging herself at Monica the way she had done after Monica had had the flu. The last thing Monica needed right now was more bruises, no matter how lovingly inflicted.

Monica had her eyes closed. Had she dozed off?

But no. Her eyelids fluttered open the moment Nicky stood beside her bed. "Hi, sweetheart," she whispered, pushing her hand across the covers and closing her fingers around Nicky's hand when Zach guided it there.

"I'm so glad you and Zeus came to help me," she said with a smile that distorted her poor battered face and broke Zach's heart.

"And Charlie, too, Mommy," Nicole said.

"Oh, yes." Monica nodded, and tried not to wince when the movement caused another stab of pain. "Of course, Charlie, too. You were all so brave. Tell him thank you for me, okay?"

"Okay."

Each word of Monica's conversation with Nicky felt like a knife was being twisted in Zach's gut. To think that he had abandoned this woman while a five-year-old girl and her puppy had offered the protection he should have been there to provide.

He would have fled the room, but since he could offer no good reason for doing so, stayed where he was.

Nicole tipped her head to the side and gave Monica's face a long and considering inspection. "You look funny," she finally declared.

"I know. Old Doc said so, too." Monica worked at another smile and Zach ground his teeth as Monica recounted what else Doc had said.

"Pretty funny, huh?" Monica asked.

But as Nicky nodded, giggling, Zach figured he'd have a thing or two to say to the doctor about his bedside manner.

Ada bustled back in with a tray. The aroma of chicken broth scented the room. "Lunchtime. Everybody out.

"Your lunches are on the kitchen table," she instructed Zach and Nicole. "You let it get cold, it's your own lookout. So scoot."

She cleared a place on the nightstand. "Nicky, Zach. Scoot..."

Monica blew them a kiss as the big man and the little girl filed from the room with uncannily similar expressions of reluctance.

Thanks to her youth and inherently robust constitution, Monica healed rapidly. Within days she was up on her feet. The swelling in her face receded, restoring its normal shape. Perhaps a little bit thinner. The discoloration would take a little longer to fade, and the fracture of her nose would leave a small bump.

She could have the nose rebroken and have that taken care of, Doc told her, but added that he wouldn't advise it. The bump would add character, he said, unless, of course, a deviated septum were to cause her trouble breathing.

Or make her snore.

Since Monica, morosely contemplating her future, figured any snoring she might do wasn't likely to be a problem, she opted to leave the bump alone.

She wondered how soon Zach expected her to pack and leave, because it had become painfully obvious to her that he wanted her gone. Ever since she was up and around again it was as though the tender, solicitous man who had spent hours at her bedside had only been a figment of her wishful thinking.

And that their tender parting—with all its implied promises—on the day Zach had flown to Seattle had only been a dream.

He avoided her. And he was merely polite and chillingly remote in his attitude toward her when their paths did chance to cross. The one time a couple of days after she'd gotten back on her feet that she had ventured into the office, he had figuratively kicked her out with a terse, "There's nothing here for you to do."

When he'd immediately resumed reading whatever it

was he'd been reading, just as though she were no longer in the room, Monica choked back her bewildered, "Why?" and had quietly walked out.

He had not joined her and Nicole again at dinner last night. And at breakfast this morning he only stopped by long enough to say, "Can you be ready to go into town in an hour?"

"Why...yes." Monica glanced helplessly at Ada who shot Zach a disgusted look that he chose to ignore.

"Can I come, too?" Nicky eagerly piped up.

"No," Zach said, so curtly that Nicole's face closed up like a flower after the sun has disappeared.

Zach pretended to ignore that, too. He had been keeping his distance from the little girl who, along with her mother, had stolen his heart. He knew that if he didn't, he'd never be able to let the two of them go.

Not for a moment did he allow himself to believe they might want to stay. Or that his chilly remoteness might be what was driving this emotional wedge between them. For the sad truth was that his need to have them in his life didn't stand a chance against his even stronger need to punish himself.

And so he had given Nicole the promised bicycle, but had thus far claimed to be too busy to help her ride it. He had told himself he was glad when he'd come upon Mitch teaching her the previous morning.

He really had been busy. He had spent the days since his return doing everything in his power to ensure Monica and Nicole a future devoid of further trauma. To get Monica off the hook before Sinclair could even utter the word "kidnapping," he had poured over legal briefs, searching out precedents that would strengthen her position.

He had also called in favors, and pulled every string at his disposal to make sure the district attorney, as well as the judge, saw things his way. Which was that Monica's so-called abduction of Nicole from the baby-sitter's had not only been justified, but imperative, since she had proof of Sinclair's heinous intention to institutionalize the child and then rob her of her legal inheritance.

Zach had also extracted assurances from the various officials that Monica would be spared undue distress when it came time to testify. And while he realized that none of this made up for his failure to be there for them, he did hope that maybe it atoned for it, just a bit.

As for right now...

"You've got an appointment with Judge Caldwell at ten," he told Monica.

"Richard?"

"What else?" Zach snapped, and quickly walked away.

Heartsick, Monica stared after him.

"Is my face still really bad, Ada?" she murmured, touching a finger to her still-tender forehead where six stitches had closed the gash she had sustained when her face had hit the floor. And her forehead the metal doorstop.

"It's not the state o' your face that's eatin' on that man," Ada scoffed. "It's the fool notions he's got festerin' in his own fat head."

"What fool notions?"

But Ada only shrugged. "That's for you to ask him, not me," she said before addressing herself to Nicky who was pouting into her breakfast cereal. "You can either sit here and make a mean face, young lady, or you can come with me to my friend Rose who lives away from here a piece an' has chickens an' rabbits an' pigs."

"Can I pet them?" Nicole asked with the instant brightening of her features Ada had obviously aimed to achieve.

"Wouldn't be s'prised." Ada motioned discreetly for Monica to leave.

Monica mutely thanked her with a strained smile. She dropped a kiss on her daughter's head. "Be a good girl for Ada."

Nicole looked up at her with a solemn expression. And rendered her speechless by saying, "Tell Zach not to be mad anymore, Mommy. Okay?"

A little while later, in the Suburban on their way into town, Monica stole glances at Zach's closed expression and was sorely tempted to give him Nicole's message. Anything to shatter that wall behind which he had retreated ever since she'd gotten off her sickbed.

That wall of indifference that made her want to shake him and demand, *Why? Why are you doing this?*

"I don't want you to worry," he said at length, grudgingly. Though he had no intention of letting her know the part he'd played in preparing for the hearing that faced her, he couldn't quite keep himself from offering some reassurance. "Doc's going to be there, too. He and the judge're old friends. He'll do all he can to make sure you get temporary full custody while permanent legalities are hashed out between the various jurisdictions."

"Aren't you coming in?" Monica asked when he simply pulled up at the curb in front of the courthouse without making an effort to park.

"No." His gaze swept her, but didn't linger. "Good luck."

He reached across the passenger seat she had gotten out of and pulled the door shut. Grim-faced, he sketched her a salute and drove off.

Crazy, but the squeal of his tires and the stench of burning rubber that accompanied his departure considerably lightened Monica's heart. Darn it, he wasn't as indifferent as he was trying so hard to make her believe.

I'll see you later, Zach Robinson, she promised him, and herself, with sudden resolve. *And then we* will *have that talk of ours, whether you think you want to or not.*

Though Zach and the Suburban were nowhere in sight when Monica and Doc Koontz emerged from the courthouse a scant hour later, Monica declined the old man's offer of a ride. She accepted his hug and congratulations, and returned his wave as he sedately drove off in his vintage Mercedes.

Alone but for a sprinkling of pedestrians going about their business, Monica tipped her face up to the cloud-filtered rays of the sun and took a good, long breath of marine air spiced with gasoline fumes and the smells of assorted fast foods.

It felt great to be alive. And, if such a thing were possible, it felt even better to be free. Free of Richard. Free to go wherever she wanted, just as long as she kept the court apprised of her whereabouts. Or...

Free to stay.

Right here. In this state. On this island. In, or rather just outside of, this town.

She opened her eyes and caught Zach watching her from only a dozen or so feet away. His face bore an expression of hunger and despair. And a desperate longing that matched her own.

Yes, she thought, it felt great to be free. To stay. With this man.

She didn't speak. She only looked back at him. Watched him as he shuttered his expression and forbade herself to be disheartened by that. She stood perfectly still as he walked toward her, and didn't move when he stopped in front of her. She only looked at him, and waited.

"Monica..." Zach's voice was rough, ragged, harsh. He stepped closer, wanted very badly to touch her. But stuck his hands into his pockets instead. "Are you...okay?"

Monica, her eyes locked on his, mutely nodded.

"Did the judge—"

"Do everything you wanted him to do?" She visibly shocked him by interrupting. "Why, yes, he did."

She could have laughed when he turned beet-red and abruptly turned away with an explosive, "How'n blazes..."

"Do I know?" She blithely interrupted him again. "Doc told me, of course. Since he apparently knew you wouldn't deem it necessary to clue me in yourself."

"Damned gossiping old..." Roughly raking a hand

through his hair, Zach bit off the rest of the muttered insult. He backed away a few steps and shot her a glare that was part embarrassment, part defiance. "I don't want you thinking it means anything."

"Too late." Daring him with her eyes to move even one more step, Monica folded her arms across her chest in a stance that clearly said, I'm not budging till we have this out. "You see, I've been thinking plenty already. And what you did *does* mean something. More than something—to me it means *everything.*"

"Then you're a fool."

"I don't think so." With pretended calm, her gaze steadfastly holding his, Monica advanced on him. "According to Ada, the fool in this relationship is *you.* Says your head is full of crazy notions. She wouldn't tell me what they are, but I think I've got a pretty good handle on them, anyway."

Only inches away from him now, she grabbed a handful of the flannel shirt his open leather jacket left exposed. She permitted nothing but confidence and conviction into her tone and expression, but her insides quaked and she silently prayed that she was going about this the right way. "I want you to get rid of those notions, Zach Robinson. You got that? Because you are not to blame for anything that happened."

"Oh, God." With a harsh sound that was as much a laugh as a groan, Zach closed his eyes and tipped back his head.

Only to have Monica grab hold of his face and gently force it back down. "I love you, you stupid man."

"For God's sake, Monica..." Zach gripped her hands and yanked them away from his face. But he didn't let them go. Couldn't let them go. Because suddenly he was afraid that if he did, she'd simply disappear, and with her would vanish his last chance at redemption. "Have you any idea..."

"You'd be surprised," Monica purred, rising on tiptoe

and silencing him with a kiss. She was both amazed and delighted with this brazen woman her love for this obstinate man was turning her into. "At the kind of ideas I've been having where you're concerned, Zacharias. Because like I said…" She kissed him again, lots of little pecks that punctuated each word. "I. Love. You."

"Monica." Zach tried one last time to object. "Don't you understand—"

"No," she cut in, growing angry at his obstinate refusal to give up and give in. Tugging one hand out of his, she gave his shoulder an exasperated little shove. "It's you, darn it, who doesn't understand."

"I understand that I don't deserve you," Zach growled with a fierce scowl that didn't even begin to hide the powerful emotions choking him up as he hauled her into his arms. "That I'm all wrong for you."

Monica's heart flipped a flop and she tightly hugged him back. She pressed a kiss against his neck. "Silly man."

"No, it's true." Zach's hands couldn't stop moving, stroking. Her back, her hair. And, very tenderly, the face she now tilted up to his. "It's been eating me up, but it's true. I've made so many mistakes…"

"Then don't make another," Monica whispered, "by turning me away." She pulled away, just a little. Just enough so that she could look into his eyes. "Do you love me, Zach?"

"Oh, God, yes. For so long now." Zach dropped his forehead against hers and sucked in a couple of ragged breaths. "It seems like forever. But you couldn't seem to see it. Weren't ready to see, I guess, that there'll never be another man who loves you as I do. Needs you as I do. But even so—"

Monica's exuberant kiss swallowed whatever final, misguided escape route Zach might have felt honor-bound to offer. She had heard all she needed to hear. Zach loved her. Zach needed her. And it was heaven.

The kiss they shared went on and on, pure bliss. But even at that, it was only a prelude to a future that was a golden strand of promises stretching into forever.

* * * * *

MEN!

A good one isn't hard to find—they're right here in Silhouette Romance!

MAN: **Vincent Pastorelli, Committed Fireman**

Look out for the woman who melts Vincent's
heart in Carla Cassidy's
WILL YOU GIVE MY MOMMY A BABY? (August 1998)

MAN: **Alex Trent, Wealthy Businessman**

Find out how Alex convinces his best friend to
open her heart in Christine Scott's
HER BEST MAN (September 1998)

MAN: **Devin Bartlett, 100% Cowboy**

Meet the woman who will make Devin commit
once again in Robin Nicholas's
COWBOY DAD (October 1998)

Available at your favorite retail outlet.

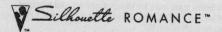
Silhouette ROMANCE™

Look us up on-line at: http://www.romance.net   SRMEN

Take 2 bestselling love stories FREE

Plus get a FREE surprise gift!

Special Limited-Time Offer

Mail to Silhouette Reader Service™

3010 Walden Avenue
P.O. Box 1867
Buffalo, N.Y. 14240-1867

YES! Please send me 2 free Silhouette Romance™ novels and my free surprise gift. Then send me 6 brand-new novels every month, which I will receive months before they appear in bookstores. Bill me at the low price of $2.90 each plus 25¢ delivery and applicable sales tax, if any.* That's the complete price, and a saving of over 10% off the cover prices—quite a bargain! I understand that accepting the books and gift places me under no obligation ever to buy any books. I can always return a shipment and cancel at any time. Even if I never buy another book from Silhouette, the 2 free books and the surprise gift are mine to keep forever.

215 SEN CH7S

Name	(PLEASE PRINT)	
Address	Apt. No.	
City	State	Zip

This offer is limited to one order per household and not valid to present Silhouette Romance™ subscribers. *Terms and prices are subject to change without notice. Sales tax applicable in N.Y.

USROM-98   ©1990 Harlequin Enterprises Limited

Don't miss Silhouette's newest cross-line promotion

Five stellar authors, five evocative stories, five fabulous Silhouette series— pregnant mom on the run!

October 1998: THE RANCHER AND THE AMNESIAC BRIDE by top-notch talent **Joan Elliott Pickart** (Special Edition)

November 1998: THE DADDY AND THE BABY DOCTOR by Romance favorite **Kristin Morgan** (Romance)

December 1998: THE SHERIFF AND THE IMPOSTOR BRIDE by award-winning author **Elizabeth Bevarly** (Desire)

January 1999: THE MILLIONAIRE AND THE PREGNANT PAUPER by rising star **Christie Ridgway** (Yours Truly)

February 1999: THE MERCENARY AND THE NEW MOM by *USA Today* bestselling author **Merline Lovelace** (Intimate Moments)

Only in—

Silhouette Books

Available at your favorite retail outlet.

Look us up on-line at: http://www.romance.net

SSEFTB

MEN at WORK

All work and no play?
Not these men!

July 1998
MACKENZIE'S LADY by Dallas Schulze

Undercover agent Mackenzie Donahue's lazy smile and deep blue eyes were his best weapons. But after rescuing—and kissing!—damsel in distress Holly Reynolds, how could he betray her by spying on her brother?

August 1998
MISS LIZ'S PASSION by Sherryl Woods

Todd Lewis could put up a building with ease, but quailed at the sight of a classroom! Still, Liz Gentry, his son's teacher, was no battle-ax, and soon Todd started planning some extracurricular activities of his own....

September 1998
A CLASSIC ENCOUNTER by Emilie Richards

Doctor Chris Matthews was intelligent, sexy and *very* good with his hands—which made him all the more dangerous to single mom Lizette St. Hilaire. So how long could she resist Chris's special brand of TLC?

Available at your favorite retail outlet!

MEN AT WORK™

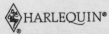

Look us up on-line at: http://www.romance.net   PMAW2

twins
on the doorstep

BY STELLA BAGWELL

The Murdocks are back!
All the adorable children from the delightful
Twins on the Doorstep
miniseries are grown up and
finding loves of their own.

You met Emily in
THE RANCHER'S BLESSED EVENT
(SR #1296, 5/98)

and in August 1998 Charlie is the
lawman about to be lassoed in

THE RANGER AND THE WIDOW WOMAN
(SR#1314)

In the next few months look for Anna's and Adam's
stories—because the twins are also heading for the altar!

Only in

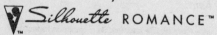 *Silhouette* ROMANCE™

Available at your favorite retail outlet.

Look us up on-line at: http://www.romance.net   SRTOD

Catch more great

HARLEQUIN™ Movies

featured on the movie channel ㎡

Premiering July 11th

Another Woman

Starring Justine Bateman and
Peter Outerbridge
Based on the novel by Margot Dalton

Don't miss next month's movie!
Premiering August 8th
The Waiting Game
Based on the novel by *New York Times*
bestselling author Jayne Ann Krentz

If you are not currently a subscriber to
The Movie Channel, simply call your
local cable or satellite provider for more
details. Call today, and don't miss out
on the romance!

100% pure movies.
100% pure fun.

HARLEQUIN®
Makes any time special ™

Harlequin, Joey Device, Makes any time special and Superromance are trademarks of
Harlequin Enterprises Limited. The Movie Channel is a service mark of Showtime Networks, Inc.,
a Viacom Company.

An Alliance Television Production

PHMBPA798

The World's Most Eligible Bachelors are about to be named! And Silhouette Books brings them to you in an all-new, original series....

World's Most
Eligible Bachelors

Twelve of the sexiest, most sought-after men share every intimate detail of their lives in twelve never-before-published novels by the genre's top authors.

Don't miss these unforgettable stories by:

Dixie Browning

MARIE FERRARELLA

Jackie Merritt

Tracy Sinclair

BJ James

RACHEL LEE   Suzanne Carey

Gina Wilkins

VICTORIA PADE

MAGGIE SHAYNE   *Anne McAllister*

Susan Mallery

Look for one new book each month in the
World's Most Eligible Bachelors series beginning
September 1998 from Silhouette Books.

V Silhouette®

Available at your favorite retail outlet.

Look us up on-line at: http://www.romance.net   PSWMEB

MATERNITY LEAVE

Coming September 1998

Three delightful stories about the blessings
and surprises of "Labor" Day.

TABLOID BABY by Candace Camp

She was whisked to the hospital in the nick of time....

THE NINE-MONTH KNIGHT
by Cait London

A down-on-her-luck secretary is experiencing
odd little midnight cravings....

THE PATERNITY TEST by Sherryl Woods

The stick turned blue before her
biological clock struck twelve....

*These three special women are very pregnant...and very
single, although they won't be either for too much longer,
because baby—and Daddy—are on their way!*

Available at your favorite retail outlet.

Look us up on-line at: http://www.romance.net   PSMATLEV